From the Hilltop

Native Storiers
A Series of American Narratives

Series Editors
GERALD VIZENOR
DIANE GLANCY

From the Hilltop

Toni Jensen

University of Nebraska Press · Lincoln and London

Publication of this volume was
assisted by The Virginia Faulkner
Fund, established in memory of
Virginia Faulkner, editor in chief of
the University of Nebraska Press.

Library of Congress
Cataloging-in-Publication Data
Jensen, Toni.
From the hilltop / Toni Jensen.
p.   cm.
— (Native storiers:
a series of American narratives)
ISBN 978-0-8032-2634-0
(pbk. : alk. paper)
1. Indians — Mixed descent — Fiction.
2. Métis — Fiction. I. Title.
PS3610.E58F76 2010
811'.6 — dc22
2010020133
Set in Minion by Bob Reitz.
Designed by R. W. Boeche.

For my family

Contents

Acknowledgments

For their faith, support, and hard work on this manuscript: my agent Kate Garrick, the series editors Gerald Vizenor and Diane Glancy, and acquisitions editor Elisabeth Chretien.

For its financial support: the Texas Tech University Graduate College, which gave me a Summer Dissertation Research Award that helped this collection along its way.

For their sharp editing and tireless friendship: Dennis Covington, Jill Patterson, John Poch, Gail Folkins, J. Marcus Weekley, Alan Rossi, Evan Bruno, Linda Helstern, Diane Warner, and Francine Ringold.

For sending me Louise Erdrich's books when I was so very far from home: Tom Hutchinson.

For the house at the canyon, for becoming my West Texas family: B. J. Gibson and her family.

For their support and encouragement: my family—Andrew Jensen, Kelly Jensen, Mary Lee Jensen, Laura Pardee, and Tim Jensen—and all those who came before.

Acknowledgments

For being first, last, always: Don and Eva.

For everything—the list so long and still being written: Stephen Graham Jones.

Thanks to the original publishers of these stories:

"Chiromancer": *Passages North* 26, no. 1 (Spring 2005), 221–226.

"Still": *Tusculum Review* 2, no. 1 (Spring 2006), 99–105.

"At the Powwow Hotel": *Nimrod International Literary Journal* 28, no. 1 (Fall 2006). Winner of *Nimrod*'s Katherine Anne Porter Prize for Fiction, 31–39.

"At the Powwow Hotel": *New Stories from the South, The Year's Best, 2007*. Series editor, Kathy Pories. Algonquin Press (August 2007), 166–177.

"At the Powwow Hotel": *New Stories from the Southwest*. D. Seth Horton, editor. Ohio University Press (January 2008), 149–158.

"From the Hilltop": *Fiction International* 39, no. 1 (Spring 2006), 151–163.

"Killing Elvis": *Yellow Medicine Review* 3, no. 1 (Fall 2007), 12–27.

"Sight and Other Hazards": *New Texas* (Fall 2006), 45–54.

Chiromancer

The redhead in the poodle skirt grabbed me up from where I hid between two giant palm fronds, dragged me to the stage, told me I was the rockabilly Indian, here to save them all. I told her I wasn't him, was just myself. That there would be no saving, that the band wasn't that bad, anyway.

By the time I moved my eyes from her, to the exit, back to her though, I was up on the stage, the drummer saying, Yeah, man, and keeping time with my steps. The redhead had her hands all over the front of my shirt, her red mouth all over the microphone, saying something loud that went out into the Easter morning crowd and bounced.

The minute before, I had been standing in the back of the hotel conference room-turned-dance hall. I was scanning around for my brother-in-law and my nephew. I was trying not to think about where my sister Linda was. I fingered the knife in my pocket, the piece of paper folded four ways. I said,

No, no thank you, no, I don't dance, to all the girls with their dark hair, which swooped down over their foreheads in neat little half moons that almost touched their eyebrows. It was like being back in time—all the guys with Elvis hair, the girls with skirts that made circles when their partners twirled them out onto the checkerboard floor. It was like being forward, too—the girls so grabby and bold, most of them as tattooed as the guys, the checkered floor just contact paper peeling up a little in the corners of the room.

With the lights in my eyes, the drums so loud behind me, I couldn't think, couldn't focus entirely on any of it. I was squinty, was hot in the leather jacket my wife Diane had made me bring. It's not cold in Las Vegas, I told her. It's cold in Minnesota, she told me, and that's where you're coming back to. She said it in a nice, even voice, but it came out like a threat somehow, anyway. That's how it's been with us for going on ten years—somebody threatening somebody quietly, somebody wearing the jacket.

The redhead with the red lips let go of my shirt to stroke the microphone with both hands. She yelled something like Viva Las Vegas, something about this being the last day of the greatest weekend ever.

I'd only been on a stage once before, and then not really on it, more like at its edge. Senior year of high school, the year Diane moved to St. Paul from Alberta, the year she asked me to take her to the prom. She didn't know that many people yet, was too pretty for most of the guys—Indian, white or otherwise—including me. Back home, her family the Roubideauxs, were famous for having pretty girls, and Diane had been homecoming queen three years running—the only métis girl to ever do that. In St. Paul, she was nominated royalty, too. My biggest claim to fame was being the fourth best-looking Indian guy in school. After my last brother Richard graduated, I was the only, and therefore, best-looking, Blackfoot. So I walked with Diane up the stairs to the edge of the stage, held her arm for her when she stepped up, and then I let go.

This time I forgot who I was for a minute, forgot to suck in my gut and turn my head to the left so my good eye pointed forward. I grinned, did a little dance, and sent out a wave to the crowd before jumping down, ducking into it. I dodged the redhead's big, reaching hands by bending forward, making myself small, and pushed my way through the kicking legs and flying skirts. I ducked and wove—moves, I had moves—heading for the lobby, out into the slots and poker tables. I feigned left and moved right, just escaping a big, pointy-toed shoe when I saw them—the short legs in blue jeans, dancing around a step and a half behind the beat. Just like his uncle. I grabbed his arm, pulled him around closer to me.

Randy, I said, where's your father?

En guarde, Randy said. He bent his four-year-old legs into a fencer's stance and brandished the sword he'd made by sticking three striped drink straws together.

Randy, I said

En guarde, Uncle Pete, he said. Who goes there?

He threw back his head and laughed at that like an old man telling his best joke. Someone had cut his hair short since I'd seen him last, and it stuck out from the top of his head, fine and electric. Two palm fronds were tied onto his belt loops. A new tradition, I guess. They fanned out behind him and almost reached the ground.

Next to us, a tattooed guy held a girl with a long skirt in the air a moment, and then she was straddling him over the checkerboard, him on a black square, her dangling above a white one, her legs wrapped around his waist. He was wearing a wife beater to show off his tattoos. A giant blue snake rose from his pale chest and circled the bear on his shoulder. Whiskey hung in the air as the guy swung the girl back and down. Her hair brushed Randy's.

Happy Easter! Randy said.

The girl laughed, moved deeper into the snake eating the bear. Randy jumped up and down, waving his sword, shaking his fronds. The girl moaned. I scooped Randy up by the waist, pulled the room key from his back pocket, and ran.

I was trying to sneak up on the room, on Randall, Senior, if he was in there practicing his Elvis, lying to some new woman. But as we moved down the hallway, closing in on the room, Randy kicked his legs and sang out, Room 262, 62, 62, over and over like a mantra. He grabbed my face with both hands, assaulting me with his little kid breath—barbecue chips and orange soda and bubble gum.

Sing, Uncle Pete, he said. Sing the Room Song.

This was vintage Randall—teach the kid a song to remember the room number and turn him loose in a hotel.

Shh, buddy, come on, I said. Let's play the quiet game now.

I made my eyes real big, aware only one was cooperating, and moved my finger up to my mouth in the *shh* gesture. Randy mirrored it, said, Shhh! as loud as possible, then drew his pudgy finger up to my bad eye. He ran his finger along my eyebrow and squinched one of his eyes down small to look like mine.

I put my ear to the door first, then my good eye to the peep-hole, which never works from the outside. Really, I was just stalling. The new knife in my pocket felt flimsy and cheap. Randy started up the kicking again, bouncing his foot off the wall. I figured we had already alerted anyone within fifty feet, so I took a deep breath, slid the card into the slot, and we were in.

Randy ran straight into the bathroom, calling, Dad, Dad, but no one answered. My breathing finally slowed, some.

The place had been trashed—Diet Coke and Orange Crush cans making a new carpet, Styrofoam containers with bits of dried food on top of the TV, the beds. I flipped the lights on, looking around for Randy's things while he jumped on the beds, fencing an imaginary enemy. I pulled open the closet door and stepped back.

An altar, a shrine of some sort. A black cloth had been hung over boxes, which were lined up like stairs. On top sat four unlit candles, a handful of rocks, a few feathers from a black bird—a crow, maybe—a small pipe, a picture of the redhead from downstairs in a polka dot bikini, a deck of Tarot cards with historic Indians on the faces, and a lock of someone's hair. New tradition number two. I knelt down, my knees cracking and popping, and took a corner of the fabric in my hand.

You're not supposed to touch that.

Randy had stopped his bouncing. He sat on the bed, sur-rounded by the take-out containers, one palm frond bent under him, one hanging off the edge of the bed.

I pulled, pulled harder, and everything tumbled. Randy ducked down behind the Styrofoam.

You're in so much trouble, he said, covering his face with his hands.

Two old gray Samsonites had been the base of the altar, with smaller, shoe-box-sized cartons on top. I grabbed the biggest suitcase. Two of the cartons flipped off it. The first held hot pink fliers with Southwestern designs on the borders, with the heading The Amazing Randall Mesteth, Native Psychic and Chiromancer to the Stars. Tradition number three, only this one wasn't so new.

When they lived in St. Paul, Randall had, for a time, been billing himself as a Native Psychic and Healer, until the night he gave Linda a black eye and nearly broke her arm. I pulled him out of the bar, into the alley behind—the first fight I'd been in since high school. He said, Not in the face, man, not in the face. I said, Heal this, you prick, but he just kept saying it—Not in the face, not in the face. Though he was Italian, not Indian, he had close to a perfect cigar box profile. He was worried about his nose. I did my best to break it before he sobered up, before he remembered he was bigger than I was.

It took me a minute, but I recognized the photo in the center of the flier—Randall shaking the hand of some celebrity, some musician after a concert in St. Paul. Diane had taken that picture. We had all gone to the concert and to the IHOP after. And then it hit me, what was wrong with it. Linda had been on the other side of the singer, had been cropped out. If you looked close, you could see her shadow, falling onto the singer, crossing over onto Randall.

I kicked the box hard, bumping it into the other carton, knocking off its lid. More fliers, turquoise, this time, with a photo of Randall in full Elvis regalia. Rockabilly Randall slanted across the top.

Hey, Randy said. Hey, Uncle Pete, want to know what your future holds?

He'd picked up the cards from where I'd kicked them, had stacked them out in front of him in three neat piles. Past, present, future, all laid out.

The door clicked open. Big Randall and the redhead fell in, laughing. The phone was ringing, Randy saying, Hello, hello, in his small voice. But I was hearing another voice under it, the one from yesterday asking if I was Pete Rampert, saying something about the Vegas police, something about an incident.

Randall had his hands up under the redhead's chin, cradling her face as if to say It'll be okay, baby. Or maybe he was saying it. I was seeing Linda laid out on cold metal, a man pulling back the sheet, tucking it up under her chin like she was still a girl. Like she was just sleeping.

I charged at Randall, swinging the Samsonite, and it glanced off his shoulder, hitting the redhead square in the eye.

Ow, she said, you bastard.

It should have knocked her out, but she just stood there, making her hand into a fist.

Hello, Randy said. Hello. He crouched down between the bed and the table, the phone at his ear.

Listen, Big Randall said.

No, I said, you listen.

I pulled the paper out of my pocket and the knife came with it, dropped onto the floor. We both reached for it. I was closer but he was faster, and he grabbed it, shoving me out of the way. I landed hard on my tailbone, my head bouncing off the wall but not too hard. Randall flicked the knife open, swiped the air in front of him, laughing.

This, he said, swiping near my nose, is truly pathetic. Even for you, Pete.

The redhead was lounging on the bed near the door now, studying her nails. She laughed, a cross between a screech and a bark. I don't know how she wasn't unconscious.

You need to sign this, I said. I couldn't forget why I was there. I had already lost once—my other sister and her husband dead in a car crash, my niece adopted out of the family, vanished. I straightened my back and waved the paper.

You need to sign this and then I'll go.

And then you'll go, huh? Randall said. I say when you go. He whizzed the knife past my nose again, getting it this time. A bad nostril now to go with my eye.

Asshole, I said. I started lurching to my feet, swinging up at him, aiming for his face, and he swung the knife at me again. I missed, but my shoulder caught his arm, the one with the knife, right at the crook of his elbow. Something popped, loud, but I didn't feel anything. We hung there a second as if dancing then fell back onto the bed with the redhead. She jumped up and was out the door fast, one flash of red, then gone.

I pushed myself off Randall. He sat up, moaning, his right arm hanging at his side, the lower part flopping.

Randy poked his head up from its space between the bed and table, the phone still at his ear. He held it out to us. The dial tone droned.

It's my mother, he said. She says you're both in trouble.

Then he started crying—a terrible cross between a dying seal and a hiccup.

Come here, buddy, I said. It's okay. It's going to be okay.

But he shrunk down even further. I looked at myself in the mirror. Blood ran from the gash in my nose down past my mouth. It dripped into the carpet, onto the paper. I wiped at my nose, picked up the paper, and waved it again at Randall, who was starting to whimper.

If you would just sign this, I said, I'll go.

But he was curled into himself now, fetal, and I didn't think he could sign anything with his arm like that, anyway. So I put the paper back in my pocket—along with one of the pink brochures—grabbed up Randy, who kicked and screamed, and ran.

On the plane, with an orange soda and peanuts in front of him, Randy calmed down some. His last-minute ticket had been $542.87. He sat by the window, looking out with both eyes as big as they could get, his mouth a small, round gap he kept putting peanuts into. I'd given him mine though I was starving, and the woman across the aisle had given him hers too. She was a mom traveling without her kids, I thought. I smiled at her and she drew back a little at the sight of my nose.

I was going to have a scar, I figured, and I didn't mind too much, but Diane wasn't going to like it. She was already going to be mad at me for forgetting Randy's clothes, for not getting the signature.

I borrowed a pen from the mom and lined it up on the tray table with the pink brochure and the other paper, the one with the x and no signature, the one that could make Randy ours. I pulled the brochure in front of me and traced Randall's signature over and over, getting the feel of it while Randy popped peanut after peanut into his mouth. We had just about found a rhythm when he turned to me.

Read my palm, he said.

He said it like I'd heard other kids say, Tell me a bedtime story—that same half-sleepy tone. He spread out his hand, palm up, and it was sticky, peanut dust in the creases.

Come on, Uncle Pete, he said.

I looked past him, out over the brown and green squares that made up everything below. I looked down at the pattern of lines curving around his hand.

Come on, he said, tell it.

I put down the pen and traced the sticky line from his index finger to the base of his hand. New tradition number four. I cleared my throat and began.

Butter

The man with the achy-breaky hair has a gun tucked in the side of his short shorts, is standing close to the young, blond policeman, who rides his horse like he's from the city. It's the Minnesota State Fair, and everyone is here to see the dairy princesses. I am here to see everyone seeing them.

I was almost a dairy princess, was runner-up in my county, which borders Canada. The whole county has only 1,882 residents, 978 of them female, 143 who are between the ages of fifteen and twenty-one, the proper dairy princess age range. Of those 143, all are white, except me; I'm an Indian, Blackfoot, the only one in the county. Of those 143, only six applied to be a dairy princess, including me. I'm interested in statistics, will major in it next year at the U. I'm interested in laws of probability. I'm interested in seeing the other girls' heads carved in butter, their real-life pictures on the Plexiglas display case above the butter ones, the case swiveling round and round for everyone to get a look.

There are crowds here, always are—people from all over, sometimes even people who look like me—Indians, like me, only they're Indians who grew up Indian, who know how to be Indian. Mom says I was not adopted from a Minnesota tribe, that only Minnesotans come to the fair, that none of these Indians are Blackfoot, are related to me. She pulls me close to her when she says it, pats down her blond hair, which she still wears all teased up, then smoothes my hair like she's trying to make us the same. This year, I've left Mom at home.

I haven't seen any Indians yet today, though. Mostly there are just white women with strollers, sweat dripping down their babies' fat arms; teenagers wearing long, baggy shorts and eating greasy cheese curds, which come in forty-two varieties at our fair; and grown men, too, lined up to look at girls' heads carved in butter, including Mr. Achy Breaky and his gun.

No one else sees the gun, not even the policeman, who is approximately 2.4 feet from the doorway. His horse keeps turning until it stops, its rear facing us, its tail haplessly swatting at flies. The policeman is here because the dairy princess display is in a Quonset hut, near the big, open, double-door exit, and sometimes the exits get clogged, all jammed with men on their way to the beer tent or women on their way to the quilting raffle. Or maybe I've got that backwards. Maybe the women are chasing down the beer, and the men are holding quilt raffle tickets, tight and secret in their sweaty hands.

My guidance counselor, Mr. Melner, says I have too many stereotypical ideas about gender, that I'm not going to become a fully developed person until I let some of these clichés loose. Never mind that I love math, am one of only two girls in my advanced statistics class. Never mind that I grew up in Mom and Dad's hotel, that I have been making beds and running credit cards through the machine since I was twelve. What Mr. Melner really means is that I should overlook how he can't throw a softball across home plate or how bright and sweaty his face gets when he mows his lawn. Mr. Melner lives across the street from me and is twenty-three. Mom says *only* twenty-three every time, right before she says, And wouldn't he make a good catch? I say he's the kind you throw back into the water, preferably with a good, strong arm. He's the kind you want to land very far from the boat.

I haven't figured out what kind the man with the gun is. He's tall, has nice muscles. The hair, of course, is a problem, and he's wearing a T-shirt with the sleeves cut off, which is how I can tell he has nice muscles. But the T-shirt is problem number two. Even so, I have to admit he's watching the dairy princesses in a way I approve of. His eyes are following them round and round, and he's not leaning forward too far like the skinny guy next to him. That guy practically has drool dripping down his pointy chin. Mr. Achy Breaky is standing a polite distance away from the case, not fogging it with his breath, and he stands back to let small children up front, which I have been doing, as well. They need to be able to dream up close.

Maybe the gun is for his personal protection. Maybe he has a crazy ex-girlfriend who is stalking him around St. Paul, around these very fair grounds. Maybe that's her, over there, with the blond braids and the snow cone. Or he could be a private investigator. In those short shorts (problem number three), he looks a little like Magnum, P. I., and I do love Magnum. There are Indians on Magnum, Hawaiian Indians, and one of them even is a detective who talks like John Wayne. I'm not sure about an Indian talking like John Wayne, but Mom and Dad love it.

Mom says I watch too many crime shows, that I read too many detective stories, that Dad needs to pay more attention to me so I don't grow up with a warped idea of what men are like. I say, Dad is fine. Dad is not the problem. He's always been honest with me—that he wanted a boy, a blond boy to take over the hotel, to give him blond grandchildren—but, even so, Dad and I get along fine. He stays out of my business. He lets me watch as much Magnum as I want. Magnum is about numbers, odds, possibilities, and I like trying to guess the end. How likely is it that the kidnapped girl will turn out to be the bad one, will pull out a gun and try to shoot Magnum? What are the odds that Magnum will rescue her, will sweep through the doors just in time to carry her home?

It's exciting, more than the games Mom and Dad watch with all the tackling and running around dumb bases. So boring it makes me want to kill myself. Mom says I have to stop saying that, that there are actual, real people who kill themselves every day. That it's serious business, Missy. I have to turn my face when she says that. It would hurt her feelings to see me laughing. And besides, I understand the seriousness. I've been depressed before, unhappy. I've watched carload after carload of people leave our parking lot, heading for their real homes, and I'm stuck in that big, old hotel with a vacuum and all those dirty towels. And then, there's how I couldn't beat out just five other girls to be a dairy princess. Talk about humiliating.

The policeman's horse wheels him halfway around. I

haven't figured him out yet, either. He's handsome enough, in a blond, boyish way, and that knocks him out of contention, I'm afraid. There are only twenty-nine brunettes in my hometown, including me, and three redheads (all in the same family). The rest are blonds. I can't wait to move down here, to the Cities, and I would never squander such an opportunity on a round-faced blond boy who is here to direct traffic, to tell cross-legged ladies where the bathroom is.

The dairy princess from my county is coming around next. She goes to my high school, is in the grade below me, and Mom calls her my arch nemesis, like we're all in some dumb comic book. Mom sometimes is seriously too involved in my life. She needs another job. That's what I think, anyway, which disproves Mr. Melner's gender theory, again. I look at the photo, Meredith Andreason in nice lighting, her dark blond hair semi-lacquered above her head, not too stiff, her eye makeup artfully applied to draw attention away from her one slightly lazy eye. And, wow, then there's Meredith in butter.

Well. Maybe I'm prejudiced; maybe I'm too jealous to judge. I'll just say that everyone around me—the soccer mom in her too-tight dress, the businessman who hasn't changed out of his work clothes—they're all taking a step back and tilting their heads to the left, trying to compensate. I'm just saying, it looks to me like the person in charge carved Meredith's head onto her neck crooked. That it's listing to the right. That her hair looks like it's sitting on her head crooked, too. Her poor hair that she spends so much time teasing and spraying and combing out afterward to avoid a super-'80s effect. Even Mr. Achy Breaky is breaching the decorum, leaning forward, tilting his head, and shaking it, too, the very picture of disbelief.

I have an almost uncontrollable urge to go to his side, to ask him what he sees. I take a step forward, and it's then that he does it, puts his hand on his gun. I take a step back. I've watched 104 Magnum episodes (that includes the variable of episodes watched more than one time), and I know enough to know that the hand on the gun means trouble. I take another step back.

Mom told me not to come all the way down to the Twin Cities, to this fair by myself. She said, You better wait for a weekend, Missy. You better wait till we all can go. Her next idea was for me to ride along with Mr. Melner, who is coming down here this very weekend.

A whole crowd of kids from school already came down last weekend, opening weekend, to hear some band. I was sensible, I thought, coming on a Wednesday in the middle of a workday to avoid the crowds, to get the best, most close-up view of the princesses possible, to make sure Mom would be stuck at the motel. And, of course, there was also the fact that those kids didn't ask me to come. I'd thought about coming anyway, about appearing at the edge of their group, standing strategically next to some good looking guy, and then I'd thought how I might get made fun of again. How I might not wear the right thing or how the guy next to me might point and laugh, and everyone would know for sure that I wasn't his girlfriend, that I was nobody's girlfriend. How everyone might, somehow, know I had tried to be a dairy princess and had, yet again, failed. And here I am second-guessing myself. I'm thinking Wednesdays are trouble, and, once again, everyone kept it a secret.

I know about secrets. For the longest time, Mom tried to

keep who I am from me, tried to pretend I was really theirs. I was twelve when I walked her over to the big mirror in the lobby, stood next to her with Dad just a few feet away, behind the counter. Look at me, I said. Do I look like you? She broke down, then, spilled it all out. That my parents were from the Blood Reserve in Alberta. That I was born over in Montana. That my parents were killed in a car wreck on the way back up to Canada. That I came to them, to Minnesota when I was six months old. That I did not belong, which I already knew.

Susie Wiggins is going by next on the display case, and everyone else is looking forward, all the heads done tilting, people rubbing their necks. I try to distract myself from my thinking, from Mr. Achy Breaky's hand on the gun, by playing the compare/contrast game. Susie's real hair, according to the photograph, is a rich, chestnut brown that the butter version does not do justice. Her smile in the photograph is a little lifeless, especially around the eyes, which stare out, half-vacant and sleepy like she just woke up from dreaming about Hawaiian beaches and men in short shorts. In butter, the smile and the eyes are both better, the corners drawn to curve up more. She seems happy, and I am happier now, too, because Mr. Achy Breaky has just returned his hand back to his side.

I take a step toward him. Maybe I do watch too much crime TV. Maybe it is affecting how I view things. Maybe I do want Hawaii too much. I don't know. All I know is that I'm inching forward, going left around a baby carriage, sidestepping a junior high boy in thick glasses, and I'm there, next to the muscles, the short shorts, the gun.

There are two more princesses after Susie, and there's the queen, of course, riding high up at the top of the case, and she will be dealt with last. I will stay in the order of their rotation, despite the natural tendency to jump to the top, to the woman who is queen. I'll keep everything in its proper place, man with a gun or not.

Next comes Bethany Wong, the butter version a nice likeness, flattering, even, her hair lying alongside her neck in small, precise waves. She looks fun in her photograph, the kind of girl I'd want to go to the mall with or to the beach on a hot day, the both of us having just painted our nails bright red, which Mom would not like. I could get away with it, I thought. With a girl like Bethany doing it, I could, too.

It's nearing the end of summer, and I've only been to the lake one time, and Meredith was there, wearing a new bikini that I had seen at the mall, that had not been on sale. I was wearing my one-piece from last year, the butt starting to get all saggy and snagged from pulling myself up out of the town pool. Otherwise, we looked about the same in our suits, I thought. Average builds, shoulder-length hair, though hers is blond, of course. Mom says it's all political, that popularity is based on so many factors other than the way a person looks, and it shouldn't work that way. That two girls who look about the same should be the same level of popular. Mom has suggested it has something to do with what she calls that attitude of yours, Missy. I think it may have more to do with my skin, and with having a mom who has so many theories about high school popularity, who insists on calling her daughter *Missy*, despite said daughter having a perfectly okay name, which is Claire.

Meredith dates a boy, Chad Simpson, who looks like he could be the blond policeman's first cousin. He's dumb, is flunking statistics, and is fond of saying things like, This shit is hard, and Dude, did you see that? The last one is usually said after he's put pencils up his nose to make himself look like a walrus.

The policeman wheels his horse around, and, facing us, he does look like Chad Simpson, I think, only a little smarter. Mr. Achy Breaky seems to notice the Chad Simpson look-a-like is facing us, too, and moves his hand closer to his gun. It rests on the edge of his short shorts, his pinky finger touching their hem, and I can feel his eyes turning from the policeman toward me, can tell he knows someone is watching him.

I turn back to the display case—soon enough, I hope—and watch the last of the dairy princesses parade by. Trista Frederickson has curly, red hair in her photograph, and the sculpting in her butter version makes several of us gasp. The lady next to me in the tight plaid shorts and matching visor puts her hand over mouth and says, My goodness.

It's true, the likeness is remarkable, the curls carved in perfect, tight spirals. In the photograph, Trista's artfully shaped eyebrows arch up and out in perfect symmetry, balancing out her smiling face in a pleasing way. And it's like that in the butter version, too.

She should keep that, says the bald man next to Mr. Achy Breaky. She should keep that forever.

A girl about my age, with long hair dyed magenta, snorts at the bald man before biting into her fried Snickers.

Mr. Achy Breaky nods, agreeing with the bald man, and I'm turning and nodding at the same time, and our eyes meet. His eyes are dark, like mine, and his hair is dark, too, and for a moment, I think he could be like me, Indian, a mixed-blood, maybe, with his light skin. I can tell right away that he knows I'm the one who was looking at him. That he knows I know about the gun. I smile, and he smiles back, and Angela Weede, the Dairy Queen, is coming around the bend. I try to focus on her photograph first, using the proper order like with all the others. I can feel Mr. Achy Breaky's eyes on me, can see from the corner of my eyes that he's smiling in a strained, unnatural way. I try to concentrate on something, start counting the screws that hold together the side of the Quonset hut, then the stripes on a middle-aged woman's blouse.

Angela looks like a queen, her dark eyes wide and bright and not overly made up. Her head is tilted slightly in her photograph, enough that I can imagine her on top of a convertible, her hand rising up, performing a perfectly executed flat-handed wave. I sneak another look at Mr. Achy Breaky. He's staring directly at me, which makes my knees threaten to buckle. Coming on Wednesday was a bad idea. I didn't check the statistics. Probably most of the fair's crime happens on Wednesdays, in the middle of the day, with nobody thinking of crime except the criminals.

I give Mr. Achy Breaky a weak smile. I'm trying for brave, and failing that, I'm going for casual. I move my arms to my sides and up above my head like all I need is a good stretch. I do a large, pretend yawn like this is all so boring, so everyday. I look at my watch to announce I'm meeting somebody any minute and where in the world is she? Or he. Maybe I'm waiting for my boyfriend, who is stuck in traffic. Maybe he looks a little like Mr. Achy Breaky except with better hair and slightly longer shorts and darker skin and without the gun, of course. Or if he has a gun, it's for official, crime-fighting purposes only and, therefore, is stowed in a more official way. Not just tucked in the side of some old shorts, which do emphasize Mr. Achy Breaky's muscles nicely, I must say. Still, it's a dead giveaway. Like Mom says, There's a time and a place for everything. And a gun in your short shorts at the Minnesota State Fair is out of place, means *criminal* or *crazy person*. This is not Hawaii, after all, no matter how nice that would be.

Angela's butter head is fit for a queen. Her eyes seem warm and still somehow convey the sense of regality that is present in the photo. Her dark, straight hair lies in a crisp bob, only the ends flipping up, just like in the picture. Mr. Achy Breaky is not watching her, is looking around the crowd, his eyes narrowing, his hand not just near the gun but on it. And then the gun is being pulled up and out of those impossibly small shorts.

I feel my eyes start to tear up behind my lenses, which are the old-fashioned, hard kind. This is the last thing I need, to have to drive all the way home in a contact-lens fog. In the doorway, the Chad Simpson look-a-like has made his horse skittish again. It titters forward, its front legs near the foot of a brown-haired toddler, who smiles at the horse and waves. I'm not so much afraid of what's going to happen—mostly, I'm afraid that all this will end. That I'll have to get in my mom's Chevy Nova, which is such a crappy, ridiculous car. That I'll have to get in that car and drive north, back to the hotel and the dirty towels and my blond parents and school starting next week. That all this will be over and I won't have seen a single Indian.

I'm thinking, deciding, my hands on my car keys, and

still, somehow, trying to get back to the place where I was yawning and stretching and being casual, and when I look over, Mr. Achy Breaky is gone, disappeared into the crowd. I'm calculating the law of averages, how likely I am to find him in this crowd, which is getting bigger and bigger with the after-work demographic showing up. I'm weighing the effectiveness of running into the crowd or staying right here, thinking surely he'll come back, surely one look at Angela Weede wasn't enough. Then, the crowd decides for me, a melee breaking out just outside the double-doors.

First, there's a popping sound, of course, just like on television, and second, there is the Chad Simpson look-a-like's horse rearing and spinning, throwing off the policeman like he's made of paper, except he lands just south of the doorway with a very real thud. His back comes down squarely on a table of cheese curds, the kind made from white cheddar, which are quite delicious, the very best of the forty-two varieties.

Some of the people run toward the double doors and the rearing horse, which makes no sense. Others, including the bald man and the woman in the striped blouse, run in the opposite direction, toward the far end of the Quonset hut. A handful of others step back a few paces and crouch down about three feet away, near the big, red-and-yellow popcorn machine. I join this group. I want to be able to see what's going on, and that doesn't include getting my eyes poked out by horse hooves.

The policeman rises, rubbing his back, which is smeared with grease. Two cheese curds linger in the middle of his shirt, right above his belt. He has his hand on his gun, is looking around wildly, telling everyone to Be calm, and to Stay down. People whisper and murmur to each other, only the babies and little kids making big sounds like wails and shouts and all-out tears. I'd like to join them but don't, of course. Mr. Achy Breaky is long since gone, escaped off into the crowd, into the Minnesota night. Unless the popping noise was a car backfiring, of course. Unless the noise, the melee has nothing whatsoever to do with Mr. Achy Breaky. This thought makes my eyes well up again, and I try to think of something happy, something fun.

Mom says this time next year, after the contest and before I go off to college, I can pay the sculptor to take home my butter head, or in the event that things go the other way, that Meredith wins again, Mom says she will find out who does the sculpting. She says she will find out, and we will send him my picture. At this point in the conversation, I say, How do you know it's a *him*?

And each time Mom smiles, says, That Mr. Melner is getting to you.

Which is *so* not true. At any rate, Mom says we'll do all this, that either way, win or lose, I'll have a butter head to display for my graduation. Of course, Mom says a lot of things—that we'll go to Canada next year for vacation, that she'll send in the paperwork to find out what ever happened to this guy, Pete, who is supposed to live around here, who is supposed to be my uncle. I want to know, too, if I have grandparents or cousins or other uncles with this name—Rampert—other people who might miss me, but Mom never does any of this.

I think she means it about the sculptor, though, really, and thinking about it here, the butter heads so close and still just out of reach, I feel myself smiling, getting calm. Of course, I haven't let Mom know this. When she brings it up, I always say, God, Mom, nobody buys one of those things, and You wouldn't want one in your house, jeez. Mom doesn't need me to encourage her.

I'm calculating the likelihoods in my head. That I'll win next year. That I'll have my own butter likeness either way. That anyone will come to my graduation party to see it. My thighs are straining from so much squatting, and my back is getting hot from being next to the popcorn machine. From here, I can't really see what's going on, can't see the butter princesses, and it's getting dark, and I'll have to go soon. A large man in a polo shirt and his wife shift their weight, huddling in front of me, blocking my view entirely. A few other people are getting up, beginning to look around. I start to rise a little, both to stretch and to see, and then there's a hand grabbing mine, pulling me back down.

I imagine, in the split second before I look, that the hand belongs to Mr. Achy Breaky, that he really is an Indian, that he's given up his gun, has risked his life and freedom to come back for me.

It's still dangerous, says the voice attached to the hand.

The girl is around my age, with dark, bobbed hair, and she is gripping my hand with a manic strength, her free hand up to her mouth, her teeth pulling on a ragged hangnail. It takes me a minute to place her, the face at once foreign and familiar. It's Angela Weede, the Dairy Queen, except her regal features are distorted with what it takes me a full forty seconds to realize is fear. Her dark eyes have become slits, her fast-moving teeth making her look a little rabbity. She tugs on my hand again, and I smile at her, give her hand what I hope is a reassuring squeeze.

Aren't you scared? she says.

Her teeth have moved from her index finger to her pinky, the rough edges reddening, starting to bleed. Her skin is darker than I remember from the picture, and with her dark eyes and hair, I'm thinking it's possible—it's possible the Dairy Queen is an Indian, is like me. Of course, it's also possible she's just tan—it is the end of summer—but I put this thought out of my head as soon as it comes. My brain immediately starts to work on the averages, the probabilities, but I won't let it. My heart is knocking around, beating much faster than its normal 140 beats per minute, and I decide—I put my car keys back in my pocket. I take both her hands in mine.

I look into her dark eyes and I smile.

This is nothing but a moment, I say, which is what Mom says sometimes after Meredith has gotten something else I wanted.

After I say it, I smile at Angela, at the Dairy Queen herself. She pulls back a little, tilts her head at me like a question. Her once smooth hair is fuzzing out at the edges, and I think about smoothing it, decide against it, think again. I don't want to be too forward. I'm thinking of the odds, all these people, and me next to her, and I'm thinking about the drive home—how tall and lonely the hotel always looks at night—and even more, I'm thinking about Mr. Achy Breaky. But I'm trying not to. I squeeze Angela's hands tighter, and say it again—This is nothing but a moment—and it seems to work this time. The corners of her mouth start to turn up a little. Just enough for her to look like her butter self again. Just enough for the both of us to look like who we are.

Learning How to Drown

I was in Raider's doghouse, my knees up under my chin. The baggy ass and cuffs of my pants soaked up water from this last monsoon rain, so when I stood up, it was going to look like I'd wet myself. I'd been brushing up against dog hair and dirt, too, me and the pants soaking up old Bassett hound smell, which was a lot like how I imagined Fritos would smell if you rubbed them under your armpits. The pants had been new, bought so I'd look impressive my last week of teaching, and were ruined now, like everything else.

Before the doghouse, there was the couch in Marana's living room, her hand on my left thigh, moving up. And last week, before the couch, there was the hotel, the getting caught. But I didn't want to think about that right now. Right now, I needed to focus on getting out of here without getting caught by Marana's mother.

In addition to being my student, Marana was also my

neighbor. Her backyard shared the alley with my backyard. On a normal day, I would jump the fence and be home in under two minutes. But my friend Joanne was across the alley, too, was in my house packing up my things, was wearing her *I'm very disappointed in you* face.

And the monsoons had been early this year—global warming and all that. The one that came through here a few hours ago had turned Marana's yard into a sloping mud hole. Marana and her mother had been in the middle of a landscaping project for as long as I'd known them. Their yard featured a border of prickly pear and yucca along the chain link, with a large, hard-packed dirt ramp in the middle that was supposed to be a small-scale buffalo jump, a sixth-grade history project nobody ever bothered to tear down.

Native people on the plains, including the Blackfoot, used to kill buffalo by forcing them off cliffs. This was what I was thinking about, to try to crowd out the other thoughts—that Marana and her friends would have been out here, in this yard, skateboarding off this ramp only four or five years ago. I focused on the history, its particulars—the cliffs almost eleven yards high, the jumps 5,500 years old. I focused on flexing my knees and inching forward, listening for the sound of the back door.

I heard Raider coming before I saw him, wheezing and slogging through the mud, spreading his wet corn-chip stench. He was old, with gray fur on his muzzle that stuck straight out, and his eyes bulged out, too, with a giant glob of snot in each corner. But those were the small details. Raider weighed at least sixty-five pounds, was almost as wide as he was long. He had sores on his belly from dragging it across the ground.

And he was loud, which became important as he waddled up to his house, put one large paw through the threshold, and touched my foot instead of the floor.

His voice came from deep in his belly, baying and howling a deep, guttural protest at my invasion.

Raider, I said, easy boy. It's me.

Raider knew me, both from the time I'd spent at Marana's house and from his own wanderings, from when he dug out from his yard and came into mine. But today he was not to be placated. He backed out, into the muddy yard, growling now in between howls and pawing the ground, throwing mud up into the air in wide, sloppy arcs.

I stumbled out of his house and fell in the mud, my feet long-since having gone to sleep, failing me entirely. Raider continued his noise. I pushed past him, willing my feet to work, and they did, sort of. If I lifted my knees high enough, I could get my feet moving forward in a stiff, formal motion that kicked up more mud than seemed strictly necessary.

This was where I was at—zig-heiling my way around the buffalo jump, Raider at my heels—when the back door opened, when Marana's mother stepped out into the yard, waving my shirt over her head like a white flag.

Bastard, she yelled. Get back here, you bastard!

I was past the buffalo jump, the chain link only a few steps away, and then I reached the fence, my muddy feet slipping and sliding and finally taking hold, and I was vaulting my middle-aged belly over the fence with surprising grace.

I'm not done with you, Richard Rampert, Marana's mother said. This is not over.

I stood in the alley, a neutral zone littered with plastic

Pepsi bottles and candy wrappers, and I was planning to say it—I'm sorry—but Marana was there, behind her mother in the doorway. She leaned against the door frame, and she had one leg up, bent at the knee. She twirled her long, dark hair with one hand. She looked right at me, daring me, the smile on her face the widest I'd seen.

I smiled with her, felt laughter rising in the back of my throat, despite my best intentions. Marana's mother yelled more loudly now. I sucked in my belly and gave her a mock salute. In return, she threw down my shirt. I waved to Marana, who examined her split ends. I was trying to convey that I'd be back, that all was not lost, but Marana yawned and headed back into the house. And now it was her mother's turn to stand in the mud, raising her knees. She brought her feet down over and over, stomping my shirt into the mud so that it was not white anymore, so that it no longer even remotely resembled a flag.

I slipped in my back door without Joanne noticing, was cleaned up and in the kitchen in good time.

Joanne perched on my stepladder, dipping a rag into a bucket of soapy water and wiping clean the top of my kitchen cabinets. I tried to look anywhere except directly at her, but I felt her eyes on me, sharp and brown and hard. Joanne and I had been the community college's history department for five years, and we were the only Indian faculty, though Joanne said *Native American*. We'd gone to bed together only once, which I said was proof I was capable of restraint, which always made Joanne snort and shake her hair in a somewhat horsy move.

Hey, I said. I'm almost done in there.

Huh, Joanne said. That so?

Yeah, I said. I picked up a plate and started wrapping newspaper around it like nothing had ever been so interesting, so important.

She was quiet for a full minute, the only sounds the crinkle of the paper, the slop of the rag into the bucket.

Huh, she said again. Five minutes ago, it looked like you still had a ways to go in there.

Joanne threw her head back and laughed, making that same horsy move, but the laughing didn't go all the way to her eyes. She stared down at me, probably examining how the thin spot on the top of my head was moving from *thinning* to *bald*.

I sneaked a look in direction, and noticed, not for the first time, how the curve of her thigh fit into the back of her knee perfectly. I thought about what it would feel like to put my hand there.

As practice, I looked away from her. I was always looking at things I couldn't have, which was okay, except, sometimes, I ended up touching them.

Joanne would have said it was that kind of behavior that got me here, packing dishes, preparing to start a job two states away, preparing for my house, *my house*, to be taken over by renters—Fred, who was the janitor at the college, and his wife Anna and their kids. They were the best I could find on such short notice, just like the job in West Texas was the best, considering. Fred was brainless and closely resembled a toad, but he was a nice man, too, solid and reliable.

I pulled the extra weight around my middle in tight, pushed my glasses off the bridge of my nose, and met Joanne's eyes. I coughed, cleared my throat, and prepared to say something to take that look off her face. But then I was saved—a car engine revving out front and something else low underneath it, something like cats mating or a door being ripped from its hinges—something low that was starting to rise.

I moved to the living room, toward the big picture window that overlooked the front yard and the street beyond. My front yard was Xeriscaped, like most in Mohave County, all of us trying to cover up the dirt so it wouldn't swirl around our houses in the constant wind. The base layer was made of tiny red and tan rock I couldn't ever remember the name of, and it was broken up here and there by a handful of smallish boulders and the cactus, of course—cholla, yucca, prickly pear, and one lone ocotillo, a transplant, who kept threatening to die. Nothing in the front yard could have been causing that noise, unless the ocotillo had learned how to scream.

Anything? Joanne asked.

The sound came again, with more engine revving this time. I pushed back the curtains, and there in the front yard sat Fred and Anna's white Buick with Anna in the driver's seat. She had driven the Buick right up into the yard, right over the ocotillo. Its spokes flailed out from under the car like a drowning man's arms.

Hey, I yelled. I was out the door, running fast toward the car, and what I saw made me swallow whatever else I had to say.

Anna's small arms hugged the steering wheel like it was the only thing holding them up. Her dirty blond hair stood on end, yet was still somehow matted into clumps. Her squinty, dull eyes were shut even tighter than usual, and tears erupted from them down her pinched face to the open, gap-toothed mouth that emitted that terrible sound.

I looked back to the house for help. Joanne stood in the doorway, a smile starting to form at the corner of her mouth, but it
stopped when the wail came again, this time with words—He's
gone. He's run off with an Internet woman.

The whole catalogue of my life's problems hung there, the
words askew, slanted, moving more than they should, almost
starting to run. I felt off balance, like I was one of those hunters
right before the buffalo jump, all of us standing at the edge of
the Porcupine Hills, getting ready to move the buffalo to the
drive lines. Getting ready for the full-on gallop to the cliff.

Joanne's guest room did double duty as a recycling room.
It was also the room her two cats liked best. Every time I
adjusted my pillow, every time I turned my head, the cats
raced across the bed and leaped onto the recycling bins, so
the cans crackled and smashed in the plastic container next
to me. It was a little like trying to sleep in a straightjacket and
simultaneously swat flies with my nose. Things had not gotten
so bad that I knew about straightjackets first-hand, but they
were bad enough that I was spending my last night in town
at Joanne's. Things were bad enough that a strange woman
was spending the night in my house, in my bed, without me
in my bed.

Not that I was interested in sleeping with Anna or anything.
Quite the opposite. It was just that Joanne made it impossible
for me not to offer. I tried. Anna sat on my sofa, boo-hooing
about Fred, about how he left her for some woman from Utah
he met online. So much for Fred being solid and nice.

We were sitting in the living room, the women huddled
together, Joanne patting Anna, and I was getting fidgety, made

to be uncomfortable in my own house. And Anna's big tear puddles threatened the leather upholstery. I had to get out of there. The skin on the back of my neck had started to itch.

I stood at the window, looking out at the ocotillo, which was bouncing back surprisingly well. I stood at the window, scratching, trying not to think about Marana—how soft her skin was, for example, or how her eyes narrowed into the cutest slits at the dumb things I said.

And I thought about stupid Fred, too, how he was screwing all this up for me. I was thinking things a nice person wouldn't be thinking. Like, could Anna pay rent with Fred gone? Could I still call in a renter-wanted ad to the paper, or had I already missed the deadline? And the women, of course, were deciding everything, and I supposed I deserved what I got for being mean, for not caring very much about Fred and the Internet woman, about all those tears. I supposed I deserved it for thinking about Marana, for not paying attention to the real problems at hand.

I came to, and Joanne was leading Anna to my bedroom.

Lie down, dear, Joanne said. Lie down here as long as you need to.

Which turned out to be all night. Joanne got on her cell phone, and it was all arranged before I could get out a full question. Anna and Fred's kids were staying at Anna's mother's, and Anna was staying at my house, in my bed, even, since the guest room had already been packed up and loaded onto the truck.

And I agreed to everything—Anna owing me less rent every month, the sleeping arrangements. Before I knew it, I was shipped off to Joanne's, to the straight-jacket bed, a good night's sleep just something I once heard about.

I flipped back and was about to throw a can at a cat when I heard it, a better sound this time, a light tap, tap on the sliding glass window. I put on my glasses, wrapping their ends carefully around my ears. I don't see very well in the dark anymore. The sound came again, a polite and insistent knocking, and I felt my way over to the window, knowing that turning on the lights could awaken Joanne and her death stare.

The yard light had come on outside, one of those automatic things that was supposed to ward off burglars. This was no burglar, of course, was instead Marana, who stood in front of the window, one hand raised to it, the other holding Raider's leash. I crouched down a little, putting Marana and me at the same eye level, and gave her a little wave. She waved back with her knocking hand, and she didn't smile.

Hey, I said. I slid the window the rest of the way open, and it jerked and hiccupped on its track like it was trying to embarrass me. I sucked in my gut a little, very aware that I was wearing only boxer shorts and a thin T-shirt.

Raider sniffed and shook his head, his jowls flapping. I was hoping he was objecting to the cats, not me, that he wasn't about to launch into more howling.

Hey, Marana said back. That woman at your house said you were here.

Yeah, I said, long story.

She nodded, looked down at her cuticles. Most women would never stop with the questions after showing up at my house to find another woman there. That was one of the things I liked best about Marana, how she accepted whatever came her way, how it took her some time to process things, but after she did, she just absorbed them, didn't cut them apart and try to put them back together in some whole other order.

Joanne would say this was one of the differences between dating a *woman* and a *girl*. Technically, no one was dating anyone here, and technically, at nineteen, Marana was a woman, not a girl, and besides, Joanne wasn't here, wasn't *here*, here, anyway, wasn't in this room. Was sleeping, I hoped, sleeping with her blue face mask and her old robe.

I thought maybe you'd left, Marana said, but the truck was still there.

Yeah, I said, still here. I made what I hoped was a funny hey-look-at-me gesture, and she almost smiled, her eyes no longer on her cuticles.

So, she said.

Give me just a second, I said.

I turned my back reluctantly, my pulse fast, sweat starting to form between my glasses and my nose. On the other side of the room, I felt around in the dark for my clothes, tried to pull on my pants too fast, tripped, and almost fell onto a striped cat. She reared and hissed at me, and Raider snuffled around outside, making too much noise.

I tried to be quiet, willing Joanne for once in her life to sleep soundly, to cooperate. Even cooperation by omission would be appreciated at this point. I was trying to hurry, more than half-expecting that by the time I got back to the window, Marana would be gone, wandered off into another yard, bored, or even more likely, that I would have been dreaming, that she was never really there the first time.

Hey, Marana said, look.

I was so relieved to see her still standing there that at first I didn't look. I was so relieved I saw only her—her wide, dark eyes, the way her shirt collar was bent under on one side.

Come on, she said, hurry.

And then I did see it. Joanne's light had come on two rooms down. She was lit up there in her doorway, her blue face all spooky, her pointy fingers punishing the phone's buttons, her eyes narrowed into that scowl. Raider started barking now, indignant at me or the cats or the lights. I stepped through the window, Marana taking my hand to steady me.

I could say we slipped away, through the dark, dark night—there was no buffalo jump to get around this time—but there was a fall, me over the bird feeder and into a puddle. I could try to make the leaving romantic, could omit the part where I stumbled into a prickly pear, the part where I got bruised and stuck with tiny prickers, almost impossible to remove. Either way, everything I've said is true. After all that, we did slip away, and it was dark, anyway, it was night.

Marana's mother worked the night shift at Mohave County Hospital, and this had been part of the problem all along. Too much time late at night. Too much access to each other with no one else around, like everything we'd been doing was just about the two of us, like it was natural and easy and right.

The college board made it clear what they thought, Joanne, too, and Marana's mother, especially. Her father had been dead for four years and, therefore, didn't get a vote, I guessed, and I didn't like to think about her father anyway, not since the time Joanne pointed out that if he were alive, he would be right around my age.

We were in the living room, both of us on the old brown couch, which served double duty as Marana's bed, and I was looking at the back door, expecting her mother to come through it any minute. Marana wiggled over, closer to me, and put her hand on my leg. I'd been thinking about restraint, I really had. About what Joanne said, about the board, my new job—Holcomb, Texas—so close and yet still so unreal.

The first time I met Marana, in last semester's American Indian history course, she was leaning back in her seat in the front row, yawning like it was six a.m., not almost noon. I lectured about Plains Indians, about buffalo hunts, and the rest of the students were leaning forward, waiting for me to satisfy all their romantic, violent expectations. Marana had her hair piled on top of her head, her eyes hardly open. After class, she'd come to the front of the room, stretching her arms and legs at the same time, a motion usually reserved for cats and small children.

Hey, she said.

This was how all her conversations started.

Hey, I said back. I was trying to be cool, to hold back feeling so out of control.

So is this class going to be, like, really hard?

She said it as if she didn't really care what the answer was, but I started to give her one, anyway, something long-winded about the reading assignments—the circular nature of Indian thought patterns, the historic battles and contemporary successes—and I could tell she wasn't listening, really, despite all the nodding, and I wasn't really listening, either, wasn't really sure what all was coming out of my mouth. I just knew I wanted to keep her there.

I'm going across the street for coffee, she said.

I was mid-sentence, and she gestured west with one hand, but I knew which place she meant. There are only three coffee shops in Kingman and only one in that general direction, the one attached to the Tip Top Motor Inn.

Still, it took me much longer than it should have to understand that Marana meant I was invited, and it took even longer for me to come up with something to say. By the time I had thought of—Hey, okay—she was giving me a little backwards wave, her skirt swishing and trailing behind her.

And I trailed behind too, that day and all the ones that followed—the Tuesdays and Thursdays, at least. We start meeting at the Tip Top after class, and what happened there was our secret, is our secret still, despite everyone now thinking they knew.

The last day, a week ago Tuesday, when I opened the door on the third knock, it wasn't Marana, was instead her mother and Joanne. And the rest was now a matter of public record—my being called before the board, my short and pitiful testimony, my quick firing. The board agreed to say they were not renewing my contract, which was different, slightly, than being fired. So I was able to call a friend of my brother Jack's, to get a last-minute job in Texas, replacing somebody with equally bad luck, I imagined.

Marana had one hand on my leg, and I sank down into the couch further, resting my head on her shoulder. I knew Joanne was on the phone to the hospital, to Marana's mother. It was such a Joanne thing to do, the only thing Joanne would know how to do. I knew we didn't have much time. Marana's hand was on my leg, her fingers drawing small circles above the precipice of my right knee, her hand threatening to jump.

After the Blackfoot chased the buffalo off those cliffs, the carcasses were taken to a camp to be treated. A young Blackfoot had been below the cliff, had lingered there to watch the buffalo thunder down. He was buried underneath them at a site called *Estipah-skikikini-kots* or Head-Smashed-In. I was trying not to think about that, though. I was trying not to think about falling or burials or anything but this moment. I cleared my throat.

Hey, I said. I cleared my throat again. Usually with Marana, I tried for young, for casual, and it felt odd to be trotting out my official voice. But I wanted her to listen, to know what I was saying was important. I started again.

You know I'm leaving tomorrow, right?

She nodded, her hand making the circles wider and wider.

Hey, I said, my voice rising. I want to tell you this.

She smiled at me, put both her hands to work on my leg.

I took them both into my own hands. Come on, I said, please.

She gave me a look I'd never seen before, and I couldn't tell whether she was serious or unhappy. Most of the time we'd spent in this room had been with the couch pulled out, watching movies until six a.m. Her mom got home at 6:30, and I had taught Advanced Civics at eight.

We've never really talked about this, I said, but you're about done with the program here, and once the semester's done, well—

Marana sighed, and I realized what her face was saying. She was looking just past her feet, was eyeing the coffee table or, more specifically, the remote control. I was pouring out my heart, and she was wondering what was on the television.

What I'm saying is that you could come. To Texas, I mean.

If you wanted to. I knew how pitiful it sounded, even as I said it.

Her hands inched forward, past my knee, making their way past my ankle—the entirely wrong direction. She groped toward my shoe, which rested on the coffee table near the remote control. I grabbed her hand, pulled it and her to me.

There is nothing on the goddamn TV, I said.

Okay, she said, God.

This was not going as expected, and then what I did expect, had been expecting, happened next, of course—her mother bursting through the door, Joanne right behind her. I looked to Marana, but I already had my answer. She rolled her eyes like this was all too much for her, and her hand still clutched the remote. My feet moved me out the door, the rest of me ducking words and small blows and minor indignities. The last sound I heard: the woosh of the TV clicking to life.

The lights were all on at my house, and Anna sat on the front porch, a cigarette at her lips, her other arm around Raider.

You have more than one of those? I said.

Here, she said, and she lit it for me.

The stars were out in full force, and everyone else in the subdivision seemed to be sleeping, their lights off, only the hum of a few random sprinklers, the distant *whish* and *zip* of traffic going by on Route 66 or the Interstate.

Hell of a day, I said. I gestured to my own porch like, May I sit here? And she nodded that I could, and it was good to be sitting, good to be home even if only for a little while.

You hear anything? I said. I was asking about me or Fred or either one, I guessed. I was mainly just trying to make conversation, to be quiet-like but not entirely quiet, not entirely alone with my thoughts.

No, Anna said, but your girlfriend was here. She raised an eyebrow at me and wiggled it, a neat party trick from her youth, I imagined, one I hoped Fred had appreciated.

She's not my girlfriend, I said.

Oh? Anna said.

Oh, I said.

She laughed a small, generous laugh, and I could see what Fred might have seen in her once. I wondered briefly how Utah was going, how Texas would be, and decided both were too many miles away to worry about right now, here in the dark.

Anything from Utah, I mean?

Anna looked straight at me, and until she did this, I would have sworn we had been looking straight at each other.

Sorry, I said. If I'm overstepping, I'm—

No, she said, looking down. I haven't heard from Utah.

We sat like that a few minutes more, her car still parked crooked out on the street, its front end nearer the curb than its back end, like someone was in a hurry. In front of it, my ocotillo didn't seem to be doing as well as I'd first thought. Its limbs drooped almost to the ground, were all splayed out, reaching down instead of up, unnatural.

Sorry about that, Anna said.

It's okay, I said. It's yours now.

I put the rest of your stuff in the truck, she said, the bed and stuff.

Oh, I said. Thanks.

I was wondering how she got the bed in the truck by herself, was about to ask, but then I thought of Joanne, of Marana's mother, and I knew the answer.

We sat like that some more, made some polite small talk, even laughed a little at some dumb joke I told. At some point I must have dozed off, because when I woke up, my head was on my knees, a comfortable enough position, despite how it must have looked.

It was still dark out, but my eyes opened slowly just in case. I had been thinking of Marana. How all we'd ever done was watch old TV shows—*Andy Griffith* and *Three's Company* and *Leave it to Beaver*. How during the commercials, she put her hand on my knee, making those circles. How when the whistling started for *Andy Griffith*, she let me braid her hair. The feel of it in my hands, in between my fingers. How this, sometimes, was enough. How sometimes it wasn't. How nothing ever jumped off from there. How it still, somehow, felt like we'd gone too far.

The sun would be out soon, rising up behind the house that was no longer mine. I stretched to the left and the right, trying to work the kinks out of my neck, the kinks that had been there for weeks, and then I heard it, a noise I didn't recognize at first, a hum that was low and then grew louder, more insistent. It was Anna, standing there with the mostly unused garden hose, on the mound of rock near the ocotillo.

That young Blackfoot who wanted to watch the buffalo go off the cliff, the one who was buried, he was much later found dead, under that big pile of carcasses. I was thinking that I was no longer young, that I couldn't afford any of this, that, in the end, I had to move my feet back from the edge. That I had to hold on.

Anna had the hose turned up full blast, was down on her knees in front of the ocotillo, was getting small red rocks in her knees and prickers from the cactus in her hands.

I moved forward, planning to tell her to stop, to say the last thing it needed was more water, that it would probably die anyway. That everything was going to be fine, really. Either way, everything was going to be fine.

And then I saw the look on her face. Anna was concentrating on something, was somewhere so very far away, working it all out in her mind, the water running between her fingers and legs and beyond her, out into the streets.

The neighbors would be up soon, and the water would still be running, out into their streets, maybe into their yards, even, giving everything another soak. And this was what I would be thinking all the way to Holcomb, Texas—how the water would be running over, soaking in or flooding. How, by morning, everything could be washed clean.

Still

The day after the third baby was born dead, the dog appeared at the end of the lane. I was sitting under the sycamore, had been there since just before sunrise. I was facing the canyon, not really looking at it, not really looking. He was as tall as a pony, with fur the color of sand. Shepherd mixed with something—dingo, maybe. He was homely and smiling and doing a whole-body wag. I said, *Tánishi*, Hello, and Your name is Henry, though I didn't make a sound. He said, That's fine, and I'd like to eat now if that's all right, and he did make sounds, but not any that could identify him as *dog*, which is what he was, I guess. They were more like horse sounds—whinnying and snorting—and I half expected him to paw the ground or sprout a mane.

I was just home from the hospital, and there was talk I'd have to go back. For observation, the doctors said. For your own good, Miller said. For as long as it takes, my family said.

The things I said to them can't be repeated here, but they were along the lines of Stop and No and Give her back. I said them in English and in Michif, though I said them with my eyes, of course, and my hands and sometimes my knees. I stopped using my mouth when the doctor held up the last baby, when I breathed in her cool, dark smell, when I could see that she never would breathe in anything.

It was just past dawn, and the morning colors splayed themselves out over the canyon. Usually I liked living way out here, nine miles from town, almost four miles to the nearest neighbor. I liked that we had Blanco Canyon in our backyard because the rest of West Texas is flat in a welcome-to-hell kind of way. Most mornings the view made me feel lucky, but this morning Henry was the only thing that seemed like luck. This morning, I was missing home, my crazy métis family, the Roubideauxs, who were scattered all over Alberta and the States now, with just me and old Aunt Bernice living down this way.

I sat there missing them too long, and the sun was halfway into the sky when Henry and I followed the light toward the house and into the kitchen where Miller stood over the sink, facing the window, his back to us. He was finishing his second cup of coffee.

This is not a good idea, Miller said. He used his cup to gesture backward, at Henry, I suppose, before running water into the bottom of it, swishing the water back and forth. Before he was finished, I knew he would swish once, twice, three times, then splash out the end of the coffee and send it down the drain like he did every morning.

I might have said, What do you know about ideas, Miller?

I might have said, What do you know about good? But not even my eyebrows were talking.

Technically, Miller's first name is Tom, but I've been calling him Miller since the fourth grade, since I came down here to live with my aunt and my cousins. Miller came up behind me at recess while I waited for my turn to kick the ball and said, Gee your hair smells terrific. I could tell he'd been practicing in the mirror for the better part of a week, wearing those khaki pants his mother spent hours ironing. I kicked him in the shin so hard my tennis shoe deflated the crease. He walked around all day like that—his left leg perfectly creased, his right one dented. Ten years later, we were married in the Methodist church three blocks from the school.

Beth, Miller said, someone is going to get hurt here.

He said it to the window, and neither it nor I replied. Henry whinnied a little.

Miller's dress shirt hung out of his pants in back, and I tucked it in for him, pulling and smoothing before reaching my hands around his middle in something resembling a hug, something resembling *please*. It was the Friday before Easter, and classes only went half a day at the grade school where Miller was principal. He was wearing his tie with the colored eggs on it. I pulled on the end of it, trying for playful, but when he turned to face me, his dark eyes were ringed, his sandy hair falling over his eyebrows. He reached his big hands around my face, his palms under my chin, and though I know he meant it as comfort, it occurred to me he could snap my neck real easy if he wanted to.

I backed away and leaned against the refrigerator. Henry snorted and rubbed his muzzle across my shins.

Beth, Miller said, but I was the one turning around now, digging into the freezer for some meat to thaw for Henry, and by the time I came out, my face was cool and Miller's truck was backing out of the carport.

After Henry had eaten four plates of ground beef and instant rice, we headed into town, to the library where I run things. My staff consists of two part-timers, Rita and Billie Jo. When Henry and I walked in, they were eating jelly donuts and smoking cigarettes over by the Westerns. Holcomb is a no-stoplight town. Like everyone else, Rita and Billie Jo had known about the baby within an hour of her passing. They hadn't been expecting me and now hurried to hide pastries and drop half-smoked cigarettes into their coffee cups before coming to rest under the West Texas field guides. They kept looking at each other, then sideways at me and Henry, then down at their fingernails. It was clear they expected me to yell about smoke and crumbs or to bawl out *I want my mother* and kick over a dictionary. Henry said, I'd like to sit under that desk, and I nodded okay, but I stood in the doorway a while, making them wait.

Just because I wasn't speaking to Miller, to the doctors, didn't mean I couldn't read to the children. They were due for story hour in twenty minutes, and I passed the time petting Henry, who was right at home under my desk. I rattled the newspaper every time Rita or Billie Jo looked my way. I liked the way it sounded, and I liked the way they jumped a little but tried not to.

After the first baby was born, the one with too many chromosomes, I read to the children, and after the second, the one with too few chromosomes, I did it again. What was I supposed to do this time, stay home and sleep? Because it was my fault this time. Because my body was to blame, I suddenly required naps and constant supervision? I expected some sort of package in the mail from my mother, an herbal remedy, something old and time-tested, something for fertility and good health, something to make a change. But instead, my mother called on her cell phone and said, *Ma-miyeu-ihkwawmiw*—that I should have a very good sleep. Like she didn't want to get too close. Like neither of our languages was up to this task.

Miller kept saying it, too, Sleep. You need to sleep. But I could hear his other ideas underneath—the *It's your fault* coming through no matter how he tried to hide it. *Sleep* was an easy enough thing to say if you were Miller, who could sleep standing up in a hurricane. Which was what it was like when the children arrived.

They were excited about Easter, had been to the grocery store with their mothers to buy last-minute candy and were all hopped up on the chocolate bunnies and marshmallow Peeps they snuck. Most of them were four years old, which is one of the very best ages, and there were no babies present though I knew a few of the mothers were speeding away with babies strapped in the backs of their minivans and sedans. I tried not to think about it. I tried to think of these four-year olds as being entirely separate creations. This was made easier when the Thompson cousins arrived.

They were blond and round-faced, cherubic-looking, but their looks, of course, were all wrong. I told Henry to watch out, and he ducked down lower under the desk, but his ears still hit the bottom of it. The Thompsons were not even all the way in the door when books started flying off the second shelf from the bottom. Rita came up out of her swivel chair in the back at a dead sprint. Henry growled, crouched lower. Billie Jo stopped smiling at Hailey Johnson, a small, freckled girl, and dove around her to grab Jack Thompson's chubby wrist. Ryan Thompson was the faster of the two, was already half-way around the library. He was squealing, which made Henry growl even more, low, from the back of his throat.

I patted Henry one last time, told him to *ekoshi eekwa*, to shush, and he did, and I clapped my hands loud, the signal that story hour was about to begin. A thin boy with glasses named Tyler Givens and that freckled Hailey Johnson both sat down in the circle first like always. Four or five other children joined them, and then most of the rest, and then Rita hauled Ryan Thompson over. I cleared my throat and smiled to indicate we were about to start.

Or at least I thought that's what had happened. Rita and Billie Jo were exchanging looks over my head, and the children, all twelve of them, shifted and wormed around on the floor as if I wasn't even there. Henry had joined the back of the circle, and I gave him a nod, which he returned. I opened the book, a new one called *The Easter Story*, with good pictures and the usual story. And I opened my mouth, too—I'm sure I did—but the children didn't seem to hear me.

I could hear them squirming and kicking their legs, and when I opened my eyes, Rita and Billie Jo had the children huddled together in the back underneath the Exit sign. And they were being quiet now, even the Thompsons. It was just Henry and me up front, and he wasn't wagging his tail; and though I asked him why—*Táneki eká wechi pékishkwet?*—he still wasn't talking.

It wasn't long before Miller showed up in the doorway, his Easter tie crooked, his hair looking like he'd just run his hands through it.

The drive home in the truck was long and quiet but was warm, too, with Henry half on my lap. He kept trying to scoot off, to curl up on the seat's middle space, and I kept pulling him back. Miller drove, looking straight ahead or out his window, so I looked out mine. I said, I'm sorry. I said, Take me back and I'll do better.

We wound through the caprock, mile after mile of canyon and mesquite, and then we were in the driveway, the truck rumbling to a stop. I said, It was the end that got me. I said, I don't think I believe in resurrections, and Miller put his head on the steering wheel. We sat like that for a while until Henry whinnied and pawed at the door, and then Miller was opening his door, and I was saying, Stop, but no one did.

I got out of the truck, ran around the side, but Henry was already gone.

Miller stood by the truck, his hands hanging in fists at his sides. He said, I can't take much more of this. He faced the truck, put his fists against the side of it, his back to me. He said, You have to talk to me, Beth. He said, You have to.

But I was already moving across the yard. I thought about going after Henry, but my legs were heavy now, and anyway, I was moving toward that other thing Miller wanted from me, sleep. And I was planning to be quiet—I was planning to be still—for a very long time.

When I woke up, it was Easter, the air heavy with rain, and I knew right away that Henry had turned up over at Jack and Lester's place, the hotel down the road. Our house smelled like ham and cheesy potatoes. I wondered how long it had been since I last ate.

Miller had my apron on, the dumb one my sister Diane had sent from St. Paul that said Kiss the Cook.

Rita called, Miller said, and Billie Jo.

I nodded and tried for a smile.

The bitches, he said, all full of fake concern. I told them you were fine, that you'd be at work on Monday. That you wanted to have a serious talk with them about their behavior.

He was smiling, dabbing at the ham with the baster, the sauce.

I smiled back, and I must have got it right because he stopped dabbing and moved toward me. I opened my mouth to say, Thank you, but my mouth was dry and my tongue felt large. Miller held out his free hand, and I took it. I cleared my throat, coughed a little, shrugged an apology. Miller squeezed my hand.

It's just us for dinner, he said. It's just us for dinner, Beth, and it's going to be fine.

Miller let me drive his truck the four miles over to Jack's hotel. Or at least he didn't stop me when I took his keys. The temperature had dropped fifteen degrees overnight; the rain was turning to sleet and might turn to snow before nightfall. I couldn't see the canyon very well, couldn't see where the road ended and the canyon began, so I slowed down to make the last turn, and there he was by the side of the road. I slammed on the brakes and slid sideways a little, but it wasn't a serious skid. I was turning around anyway, heading back to the spot, telling myself it was a coyote. Somebody hit a coyote, that's all.

But once I was out of the truck, it was Henry, of course, his eyes blank, tongue hanging out, his fur matted with what I kept telling myself was rain. I put my hands on his side, but nothing happened, nothing moved, and I knew that's how it would be.

That's how it was with the third baby. I woke up one day in the twenty-sixth week, and she had stopped moving. I had been calling her Laura, after my mother, even though Miller said not to. He was worried about the chromosomes, everyone was, including me, but Laura was born fine that way. It was me this time—something none of us anticipated—something about my antibodies. And everyone, one more time, saying how we could try again.

The hotel was dark, and I was glad. Jack had lost his wife Charlene not too long ago, and their son, Lester, had lost his mother; they didn't need to see this on the way back from church. I figured Lester was growing fond of Henry already, was calling him something goofy like Germy, as in Germy the German shepherd. I made a face, thinking about it, and shook my head.

Henry was not as heavy as I thought he might be. I was trying not to look at him as I put him into the back of the truck, was trying to think ahead, hoping the rain would make the ground soft. I was trying to be grateful for the rain. This time of year, before the heat of summer, we couldn't get enough, and it would make digging the hole easier. I could see Miller leaning into the shovel, turning over the ground like we did each spring for the tomatoes and peppers and okra. And I wanted his help with this digging, too—I did—but I wasn't sure what to say. And I wasn't sure I'd be able to ask.

It would be time for planting soon enough, time for

wildflowers in the canyon and yucca blooming yellow and purple at the edges of the yard. And that was where Henry should go, where we should put him.

It rained even harder on the way home, and I pulled the truck into the carport so Henry could stay dry. I knew in order to get Miller out into the yard, into the rain, I would have to tell him, to speak. I looked out toward the canyon, then back to the house.

I could see Miller at the kitchen window, bent over the sink, scrubbing a pan, maybe. He liked to do the dishes as he went, and I liked to stack them up in a big pile because he couldn't stand it, the chaos, the possibility of a big, loud fall.

I turned the truck's lights off, and there in the dark, I practiced. First, I said, I'm sorry. Then I said, Henry's dead. It was bad to say his name—I knew that. I knew I could be calling him back, and a part of me wanted that, a part of me waited, looking out the windows toward the canyon, but no one came.

I practiced some more, had to try twice before *dead* came out right in English, and I couldn't say it at all in Michif, couldn't find the right words, though I asked, *Tawnshi eh itwayk awn Michif?* But no one came, no one answered. Then, I said, We're going to stop trying now. I said, This is the last time.

I said, It's time to eat the ham, so we did. The potatoes, too. And we talked about the garden, about having more tomatoes this year. You can never have too many tomatoes. I practiced, said it all once more, in English, and as best I could in Michif, too. And I was looking in the mirror this time, to make sure my mouth was behaving, but it was growing darker outside, and I sat there like that a while, my hand on the doorknob, my mouth a very long way from the mirror.

At the Powwow Hotel

When the cornfield arrived, I was standing in our hotel's kitchen, starting Lester's birthday cake. It was raining outside, foggy, too, for the sixth day in a row, and there was flour all over my blue jeans. I was trying to figure out what the book meant by *sift*. Lester had been outside by the canyon all morning, inspecting bugs or digging holes or looking into the sky. But then he was in the kitchen, looking up at me, saying, Dad, it's here, his hand on the dish towel I'd tied around my waist. Lester had only spoken about ten words since his mother died last month, so I put down the flour and followed.

We live in West Texas on a three-hundred-acre cotton farm at the edge of Blanco Canyon. We own the Blanco Canyon Hotel, all twelve rooms, though everybody in town calls it the Powwow Hotel on account of Lester and me being Indians, Blackfoot, more specifically. My wife Charlene, she was Indian, too, Comanche, from around here. There had never been a powwow out here to any of our knowledge, but that's just how people are in West Texas—what they know about Indians involves the Texas Rangers, powwows, or pictures of Quanah Parker they've seen in bars and restaurants, way in the back by the bathrooms. We were never sure whether to ignore the joke or to capitalize on it, to change our name and market ourselves that way. We talked about it, Charlene and me, laughed over it.

But there hadn't been much laughing lately, with it being just Lester and me, with Lester not talking and getting picked on at school for it. This kid had said, Hey, Lester, I hear your mom died. I thought all you Indians were extinct already? And then, according to his teacher, most of the other boys in the class laughed. She said the kid who said it was a bully, that the other kids were afraid. But I said when I was in school, fourth grade was when kids started to get mean, that I couldn't imagine things now being too much different.

It was late fall, just before Thanksgiving, and most everybody had their cotton in, except for a few late fools who now were having to wait out the rain. Out here, where we live, it's four miles to the nearest neighbor and nine miles in to Holcomb, the nearest town. It was a record rain year according to the papers and the blonde girls with big smiles on the TV. Lester followed the weather on the Internet, had been writing in his journal about the rain—how we were over five inches for the month, how the conditions might be right.

Lester was supposed to be using the journal to write down how he felt, what with his mother being gone and his not talking much. But mostly he wrote about the weather here in Texas, and north of here, all the way up to Canada. It worried me, this obsession, because the only jobs I knew of where you got paid to think about weather were on the TV, and they involved being smiley and blond and a girl.

Lester still had a hold of the dish towel, was pulling me toward the western side of the property to the grassy area in between the canyon and the biggest cotton field. He stopped about twenty feet shy of the grass, his face turned up to mine, his eyes the size of silver dollars. At first, I thought the grass had gone crazy, what with all the rain. But then, through the thick fog, I saw something waving above my head, something tall and green but not like grass. I stepped forward, kept stepping forward though my heart stuttered and my throat went dry. I kept stepping forward until I was in the middle of it, touching its rough edges, stalks towering over me, next to me, short ones, too, some only knee-high. I was standing in the middle of it, breathing in the new smell—green and raw and still like dirt, somehow—when I felt his hand, on my arm this time.

Dad, Lester said, they're going to be here soon.

And he led me back out of the corn to the hotel, and we started to prepare.

The first carload of Indians arrived two hours after the cornfield. Lester and I had spent the time making beds and sweeping floors, clearing the dust off everything as best we could. November was never a busy tourist month, not like May or June, and we hadn't had any guests since Charlene died, since the rain started turning the caliche road into wet cement. The whole time Lester talked about the cornfield—how it had started showing up in Canada, on the reserve north of

Selkirk last spring, how it had been traveling south ever since, how along the way, Indians had been following.

How come I haven't heard about this? I said.

Lester rolled his eyes, which were still large, almost all dark pupil, and he shook his head at me. His dark brown hair fell into his face, and he pushed it behind his ears, all business. Dad, he said, you only read the Lubbock paper. He snickered. And you watch the local news.

We went into his room then, and looked at his computer for a while, and he showed me the places where people were talking about the corn.

The meteorologists, the scientists, the ones who believe it exists, say it's global warming, Lester said. That it's all the rain bringing it.

I nodded like I understood.

But a lot of scientists say it's just an Indian trick, Lester said.

I nodded again. This I understood. And what are the Indians saying? I said.

A car honked out in the lane. We looked out the window, found an old Buick, its tires caked with the cement-like caliche, its side splattered. Five people were pulling themselves from the car, stretching and laughing and moving toward the corn.

Lester was already at the door when he turned to me.

Dad, he said, you can ask them yourself.

The first family, the Jenkins, were from Alberta, from the Blood Reserve, and they had been following the corn since the beginning. Melvin Sr. knew my uncle Jack, who I was named after, and we shook hands out in the muck of the caliche lane, grinning at each other, then looking down at our feet, then back up at the corn.

It's something, Melvin said. He hitched his pants back up to the middle of his belly and rubbed the top of his head. He wore a buzz cut, ex-military, maybe, and his nose looked like it had been broken at least three times. He was well over six feet, a half-foot taller than me, but standing next to him didn't make me feel short. It made me feel like I should stretch a little, should try to be taller.

Yes, I said, it's something.

I wished Charlene was here. She was the one who knew how to talk to people. Lester and me were a little pitiful that way, although today Lester seemed to be doing better than I was. He was over in the corn with Melvin Jr., and even through the rain, the next car pulling up, honking, I could hear them laughing.

After the Jenkins, the cars came one behind another and pickup trucks, too, and then the news crews, of course, and the anthropologists. The last anthropologist's old truck bogged down in the caliche half a mile in, and carloads of Indians drove by, honking and waving, leaning out their windows to take pictures, yelling, Don't worry, we'll document it for you. But somebody picked the guy up, eventually. He was here in time for dinner, for the extra place we'd set at the picnic table.

By dinnertime, the rain had finally calmed down to a drizzle. Later, it would stop altogether. Almost everybody had brought their own food, and those who hadn't were fed by Lester and me or by someone else who'd brought enough. Some

Lakota named Artichoker flipped hotdogs and hamburgers on the grills, which had been set up under the tallest sycamore. The Jenkins helped pass out paper plates, and a group of middle-aged and old women had taken over the kitchen inside. Someone had finished Lester's cake, and a big group gathered around, singing, and Lester blew out all ten candles in one try, which seemed like good luck.

Our neighbor Tom Miller drove the four miles over from his place and brought an extra picnic table. He worked in town at the school, but he also worked part-time for the *Holcomb County News and Chronicle*. He brought along a notebook, but his camera was broken.

Shit, he said. I didn't know there were this many Indians. He ran his hand through his gray-blonde hair and stared.

He was so busy looking at all of us that I wasn't sure the cornfield ever registered, not really. He went around interviewing people, asking just a few questions at a time, mostly where were they from and what did they think of Holcomb County, of our fair state?

I was busy running around with a garbage bag, picking up Coke cans and paper plates when I saw Tom trying to back his truck down the lane through all the chaos. He rolled down his window when I came over.

I suppose your competition will be here soon, I said.

Doubt it, Tom said.

Oh?

I called it in, Tom said, tried to stir up some interest, but the Lubbock editor said he didn't think their readers were much interested in Indians. Indians or corn.

Oh, I said. Well.

Good for business though, Tom said, gesturing at the crowd.

Yeah, I said, good for business.

He thumped the side of the truck with his hand, gave a little wave, and weaved his way down the lane.

The stars came out thick, with the canyon underneath, and those who were going to be sleeping outside joked they had the better lodging, the room with a view. The twelve rooms inside were taken up by the Jenkins and the Artichokers, another Lakota family called Blackbonnet, some Anishinaabe named Bairnd, a Laguna Pueblo called LaLee, some Navajo named Richardson, a Cherokee family called Jones, two Hualapai newlyweds named Whatonome, a Choctaw named Byrd, the old métis Mrs. Roubideaux from in town, and the anthropologist, Becker, who'd called ahead from his broken down truck and snagged the last room.

On the back porch, a Navajo and an Aguna Pueblo were talking about why the corn had skipped them, had set its course east of their tribes.

We're from corn tribes, right? the Navajo said.

I know, said the Laguna Pueblo, shaking her head. Maybe it'll change course, come our way next.

This was the favorite conversation, of course, predicting where the corn would go next or guessing how long it might stay. According to the Jenkins, its average stay in one place was only forty-eight hours. Just like the average hotel visitor. Just like the time between Charlene's diagnosis and her death.

Melvin Sr. and I took over the porch after the women from Arizona went inside, and we sat on opposite sides of the porch swing, letting it move a little but not too much, looking out at the people setting up their tents in front of the corn, the canyon. I couldn't see the corn that well, but I could hear people moving through it, the rustling of them against the stalks like candy wrappers being opened, a good sound, full of expectations. There were even some people with bedrolls and sleeping bags who liked to sleep in the cornfield itself, right there with the itchy stalks and that bright green smell.

I'd been thinking about what Melvin had said—only forty-eight hours—thinking about Lester, who was in his room playing with Melvin Jr. I'd been wondering if there was any way to prepare for it leaving.

Melvin, I said, is there any way to know? To know when it'll be gone?

Nobody ever sees it, he said. People have tried, but it always goes at night, comes to the new place before dawn.

Angela, Melvin's wife, came out of the kitchen, bringing the smells of coffee and baking bread with her.

Those boys are going to want to sleep in the corn, she said. That all right with you?

She was asking me, but she was smiling at Melvin, her arm moving up and down his back. I looked away. Over in the cornfield, flashlights blinked and flickered. The scientists were examining its root system, Melvin had said, trying to figure out how it attached and detached.

Sure, I said, that's fine. I'll go tell them.

When I walked through the kitchen, the women were cleaning up. They got quiet for a moment, the hum dying down, and all I could hear was the whir and hiss of the big coffee pots. The smells of coffee and soup and baking bread were making my mouth and eyes water, even though I was full. It hadn't smelled like that in our house in a long time. Charlene had only been gone a month, but she hadn't been herself, hadn't been cooking for a long time before the doctors said it out loud, cancer, before the last quick days and the long quiet after. I realized I was just standing there staring, that I was making the women nervous, so I passed through, and they started up their talking again, and everything sounded right.

Lester and Melvin Jr. were in Lester's room, studying the computer, their heads together, talking soft.

Lester, I said, it'll be time for bed soon.

He turned around fast, startled, but he still smiled at me. He and Melvin exchanged a look, and Melvin grinned.

Okay, Dad, Lester said. That's fine.

He and Melvin were laughing when I backed out of the doorway, and I had the feeling they were laughing at me, something I'd done or said that I didn't know about, but that was fine with me. Any kind of laughing was fine with me.

The next morning arrived bright and clear, and by the time I was up, the women had taken over the kitchen again, or maybe they'd never left. Either way, they were fixing cereal bowls for the boys when I came downstairs, and I carried the bowls out to the cornfield, calling Lester's name as I went. He and Melvin Jr. were lying face down in between rows of corn, examining the roots with a magnifying glass. When they rose, they looked serious.

What do you think? Lester asked.

I opened my mouth, but then I could see he was talking to Melvin Jr., so I shut it again.

You might be right, Melvin said.

No, Lester said. No, no, no, no, no.

And he was off, running past me and the cereal bowls, the corn fronds opening for him, then closing behind.

I found him in his room, clicking away on the computer, his eyes narrow and tight, his mouth a line there'd be no arguing with.

Hey, I said. I set down his cereal bowl. It's going to get all mushy.

He ignored me like I figured he would, and for the thousandth time, I wished for his mother. Charlene knew how to joke him out of his moods, knew when to back off or step forward. I had retreated to a space halfway between Lester and the door.

Lester, I said. What's—

Go, he said. Just go.

After breakfast was served and the sheets put in the washer, I cornered Melvin Jr., who was bouncing a super ball off the side of the house.

They've moved a sixteenth of an inch, Melvin said.

What? I said.

The roots, he said, they're starting to move.

Lester spent the day in his room on the computer, tracking the weather patterns, praying for rain. The sun here was so bright the paler Indians were applying sunscreen, the blondes in particular. A group of teenagers played hacky sack, another tossed around a Frisbee, and a large group of Choctaws started a game of softball that went on past lunchtime and only ended after dinner when the sun started setting, sinking red and orange and yellow into the canyon.

I was on my way into Lester's room with a plate of hotdogs when I saw Angela in the doorway. I stepped around the corner, leaned into the wall, trying to hear, but I couldn't. It wasn't long, though, before the two of them came out, Lester looking less angry, holding a hotdog in one hand, his magnifying glass in the other. And it was then that I heard it: drums starting up low, voices rising alongside the drums.

By the time I weaved through the women in the kitchen and got back outside, the dancing had started. No one was in costume—no spare room in the cars, I guess—but everyone was moving anyway. Old women stepped forward in time with the music, their hands clutched to their chests, though few held fans or shawls, and some had their hands hanging down, keeping the rhythm at their sides. Teenage boys and girls were leaping and falling in blue jeans and T-shirts, the drummers speeding up or slowing down, trying to make the showoffs miss a step.

Melvin nodded to me, and I went over to the edge of the circle, stood next to him.

Say *hi* to Uncle Jack for me, I said.

Sure, he said. Anything else?

Tell him he missed it, I said. Tell him he missed a hell of a show.

Lester was across the circle from us with Melvin Jr., and beyond them, some people were packing up already, anticipating the morning. Angela finished up in the kitchen and made her way over to us. Some teenagers at the edge of the circle were drinking from liters of Mountain Dew, sliding little pills into the sides of their mouths like no one could see if they did it that way.

They're trying to stay up, Angela said. Trying to stay up to catch it moving.

I leaned forward and turned my head a little, listening for the corn, but there were only the sounds of the drums and the laughing and the feet pounding. I leaned forward further, squinting, but it was too dark, and I couldn't make out where our yard stopped and the cornfield began. I could still smell it, though, even if it was a smaller smell now, less green, less bright.

What did you say? I asked Angela. What did you tell Lester?

She sighed and looked out over the crowd. I told him this is it, she said. I told him he could wait in his room all he wanted, but that his mother wouldn't want him to miss this. So much has been taken, but I told him to look—to look at what we have.

I nodded.

And I brought a hotdog, she said. That helped.

We laughed, and Melvin joined in. Across the circle, a tall, skinny girl took Lester by the hand, and a shorter, plump one grabbed Melvin Jr.

Hey, Melvin said, look at that.

Melvin Jr. and the short girl were swept up right away, into the counter-clockwise stepping, both of them keeping good time. Lester held back at first, pulling away so hard that the skinny girl's arm looked like a rubber band that might snap. She started to walk away, and I held my breath. Go, I wanted to shout, go on, Lester. She was three steps away, headed toward a large boy to her left, when Lester started to move. It was slow at first, like he was having to tell his legs to go, but soon he caught up to her, was tapping her on her bony shoulder, and she was turning.

I breathed out, and I thought I heard Angela and Melvin doing the same.

Angela took Melvin's hand and pulled him a step toward the circle. Come on, she said, dance with your wife.

Lester was keeping rhythm better than I would have guessed, was matching up with the skinny girl's long strides. They moved past me, and the skinny girl leaned down to say something in Lester's ear, and Lester laughed and said something back.

In the morning, the sun would still be shining. I knew that. In the morning, a quiet was going to descend that could expand, could make that other quiet grow in a way that would bring on even more sadness. I knew that, too. But tonight, there was the sound of feet, moving counterclockwise, the smell of coffee and bread and the raw, greenness of the field. And tonight, there were my legs, too, stiff at first, but surprising me by doing anything at all, and then there I was, part of it, moving.

From the Hilltop

If the hotel roof had been any hotter, if it had been any higher, if I had fallen, too, or instead; if Bean had officially died, if we had been drinking less or more, if there had been more than one girl there, if there had been fewer than us four guys, if we had all listened to Jeffrey, who is a biology professor now, the only one who got out, who was always worth listening to, who was hated, a little, for it

If we had hated less, had *been* hated less, if there had been more Indian kids in our town, not just the five of us, if we had cared less about being the only five, or more about school or horseback riding or making our own comics or anything other than perfecting the art of not caring, of slouching against the wall outside the low-slung school, if Bean hadn't been my brother, if he hadn't been the youngest, if he'd learned to walk hard like I taught him, to sneer and scowl and stuff it all down, if he hadn't worn those dumb, falling-off-his-ass pants, if it hadn't been the '90s, those pants not yet cool, if they hadn't been so good for hiding things

If Roy hadn't once loved Gloria, if Gloria hadn't been our mother; if Roy had taken us camping again, like he said he would, if it hadn't been so hot, if there hadn't been that argument about frying an egg, if we'd chosen *sidewalk* over *rooftop*; if the Hilltop had not been so tall, calling us; if there hadn't been the question of the egg, if we had stuck with smoking pot, if Mandy hadn't moved in next door, into the bad-luck house, with its four small rooms, its cracked windows, its foundation full of fist-sized holes, its refrigerator holding only baking soda, the two eggs, then Mandy, holding the eggs out, one in each palm, if Bean hadn't said, I'm going to marry her; if he hadn't been just twelve years old, most of us older, fourteen, if we hadn't all laughed—even Rick, who was Bean's age, his best friend—if Bean hadn't had to prove us wrong

Because it was my mom's house we stole the beer from, because there was wine, too, Boone's Farm, and a fifth of Jack Daniels that Roy had hardly touched, because my mother had boxed it all up, neat, had set it on the front steps in the hot, white West Texas sun, because it was hot too early, only May, school out in less than a week, because we all itched—summer so close—because Mom said, No more, to Roy, our stepfather, because he had slammed the door for maybe the last time, because she picked up her books, the ones from up north, with the pictures of people she called our people, Blackfoot

Because she watched our stepfather leave, pointed to the books, to the language none of us knew, said, This is what we're going to do this summer, because Bean had never known our father, never known any of the Ramperts very well, because Bean followed Roy out onto the front porch, into the blowing dust, because Bean watched the pickup door slam, the tailgate bouncing and jerking down the rutted street, past yucca and prickly pear and lawns there was never enough water for, past plastic bags snagged by tree limbs and fence tops, past pit bulls running the streets, dragging thick chains, past the park someone had forgotten, half its grass as tall as Bean, the other half brown and scorched and never coming back, past families playing in their yards, past our school to the stoplight, then the last hope—a brake light—because Bean held his breath, me behind him wishing he would just goddamn breathe, because Roy and the truck bounced onto the highway, because we couldn't rid our ears of the ring and bounce, that slamming door, because Mandy was holding out those eggs, because the box was there

Given that I didn't want to sit in the house all summer, given that I didn't want to learn what Mom kept saying was *my* language, given that I didn't want to learn anything at all, given that the night before I had kissed Mandy behind her house, both our mouths open, tongues out, given that Bean was in his room, given that the sun hadn't quite dropped, given that there was still enough light, given that Bean's room, its window, faced Mandy's yard, given that he then stopped speaking to me

Given that Roy had packed both suitcases this time, had taken more than just his old clothes, the ones he wore in the cotton fields, given that Roy had left his gun, given that I didn't know this yet; given that Jeffrey and his little brother Rick appeared on the porch, Rick with his boom box on his shoulders, both of them seeming to rise out of the dust that would soon be a storm, given that Mom backed into her room, holding her rosary beads, closing the door softly behind her, given that Bean had picked up the box Roy left, given that Mandy was there now, too, her dark brown hair not tied back, screaming around her head in all that wind, given that she was moving her hands, pretending she was going to juggle those eggs, given that I let the screen door slam behind me, that I said, It's not hot enough, and Mandy said, Is, too, and Rick nodded, grinning his uneven grin, agreeing with Mandy just to piss me off, even Jeffrey playing along

Given that I took the first step, started walking west, toward the Hilltop Hotel, the highest point in town, Bean next to me; given that the box was too wide for Bean's short arms, given that he started to bobble it, given that I was there to catch it, to prop up its other side

When the hotel had been four-star, when Holcomb still had oil, when most of its citizens had good-paying jobs, when J. P. Holcomb made his first million, then his second, when he decided he wanted to build the tallest building for two hundred miles, that he wanted to live on its top floor, man after man coming from Mexico, bringing their families, laying six stories of bright red brick under the same white hot sun

When those families stayed, when J. P. Holcomb started locking up his car, when the oil dried up and Main Street closed, store by store, when J. P. Holcomb barricaded himself in, way up high on the sixth floor of that perfectly square building, when everyone started blaming the immigrants, saying they brought bad luck, when J. P. fell from a sixth-floor window and the Hilltop was said to be haunted, when the bricks started to fade, when it closed down until another Holcomb, R. T., brought cotton to the area, which took all the water, which was unnatural; when the jobs started to come back, when R. T. opened up the hotel and took over J. P.'s room, when R. T. died, left the room and hotel to his son, R. T. II, who lived in New York, who sold out, who left the Hilltop vacant for us

When I learned all this, later—after; when we arrived at the Hilltop, driven by the same things as the Holcombs, need and heat and desire and the almost unnamable thing that is hope, maybe; the thing that makes us believe we can outrun bad luck

Before the Holcombs, the pioneer settlers, and before them, the Comanche, who are still here, of course, Mandy included; Mom liked to say, Don't forget, you're standing on Comanche land, and then one of us would run over into Mandy's yard, start war-whooping, which got the rest of us going, and then Mom slapping the backs of our heads, Mom sighing

Before the Comanche, of course, no real record; before that and after—sagebrush and yucca and high winds and high heat and dumb teenagers, climbing

With the hotel's back windows boarded up, nailed shut, up to the fourth floor, with the fire escape missing every other step, with my legs being the longest—arms, too—with Mandy saying, What are you, chicken, like a statement, a foregone conclusion, not at all like the question it should have been, her eyes flat, her hair still flying and tangling

With Bean kicking at the hotel's front door, Jeffrey pulling on his arms, Jeffrey and Rick finally picking Bean up, carrying him around back to the alley, Jeffrey saying, Not now, man, and This is not the time; with Jeffrey pulling the small pipe from his pocket, looking around the alley, just garbage bins and thigh-high weeds and graffiti on the sad, faded brick—*Jenny does Joe; Joe does it better; Jenny does Joe and Don*—with Jeffrey giving the pipe to Bean first, Bean taking it, breathing in, holding in, looking at me for the first time all day, his eyes the color of standing water, what Mom called hazel, her pretty, hazel-eyed boy, till he let her know he was too old for *pretty*, for *boy*

With those eyes on me; me saying, *I'm sorry* back with my eyes, me trying not to look at Mandy, Bean handing the pipe over to Jeffrey, who leaned against the faded brick, Bean not handing the pipe to me, then to Rick next, then to me, last; Bean still watching with his mud-puddle eyes, me taking a hit, and a cat, orange, striped, bursting out from behind the trash bin, all of us jumping then ducking down, laughing but not hard, relief like summer, just out of reach

With the stairs being narrow, the side rails weak and loose, with my lungs burning, with the sense of falling backward, what I will later learn to call *vertigo*, with the rock in my left hand, the pipe in my right, with my crazy balance I will later wish Bean had, with my fourteen-year-old bravado, with my thighs burning, with the top almost there, then there, with the pipe now in my pocket, with the rock wrecking the window, the glass making its falling-in noise, with my feet on the fifth floor, Bean and Mandy and Rick and Jeffrey below me, jumping and laughing and high-fiving

With the building splitting the sun, it sinking, with the dark coming on, regular, like it has a right to

Aside from the way the floorboards sank and gave a little under me, aside from the cobwebs, the relentless dark, aside from the way my heart performed off beat, aside from the lack of the big flashlight, which we used to spotlight raccoons out in the country sometimes with Jeffrey and Rick's dad, the spotlight which was far below, waiting with Bean and the others, aside from my eyes taking time to adjust, aside from my remembering—Bean at five, me at seven, our first and last camping trip with Roy and Mom, setting up our tents in the dark, no one bringing a flashlight, Roy saying, Grady, this is your fault, and Bean joining in, Mom silent, me the next day, checking my list, finding no *flashlight* there in Roy's bad, left-handed scrawl, me knowing *flashlight* was on Bean's list, Bean knowing, Roy knowing

Aside from the small cuts on the backs of my arms where the edges of the window had got me, aside from the crunch of the glass into hardwood, aside from my eyes adjusting, the chandelier overhead, its arms waving, the feel of the walls on my fingertips, smooth and cooler than I would have thought, feeling to the left where the door might be, inching along, taking my time, knowing Bean and the others were below, waiting at the back door, shuffling foot to foot, ducking down at the slightest noise

Aside from the doorway, which was without its door, and the hallway, and the railing, better than the one outside, aside from how I knew I should take the stairs down, how I knew I should not go up; aside from my hands, reaching up the railing, my legs following, the sixth floor one short flight up

Once I'd started up the stairs, tripping and stumbling twice, once on the sixth floor, once I remembered the pipe in my pocket, the lighter, once I'd laughed and cursed myself out, once the flame was going, once I'd made my way to the double-doorway, its doors the tallest I'd seen, twelve feet, maybe, with curlicues at the top that looked like a woman's hair, once I'd stopped thinking about Mandy, out in the alley with her soft mouth, her dumb eggs, once I'd opened the doors, the brass handles pulling hard, once I was in Holcomb's room with the cobwebs and spiders and the ceiling, which made me have to close my eyes, to have to sit down in the middle of the room, dizzy

Once I'd lit up, my eyes back open, the lighter flickering, once I'd narrowed my eyes and looked closer, the ceiling: tin, maybe, or silver, something that color, anyway, and probably shiny at one time, and people carved out of it or into it, once I looked closer, once I could see what they were—dancing people, some with wings, large, feathery wings, outfits like I'd seen on some fancy dancers one time at a powwow over in New Mexico—once I thought about how these couldn't be fancy dancers, were angels, maybe, or something like angels, once I closed one eye, squinted, decided they could damn well be fancy dancers if I wanted them to

Once I'd gone to the famous window, stood in J. P.'s place, looking out over the lights of the town, all the way to Lubbock, really, where there were now buildings taller than J. P.'s, once I leaned my head against the glass, realized I was sweating, once I took a breath, heard the banging below and the voices, Mandy's giggly and high, Bean's the loudest; once I could tell they were into the liquor, already loud and reckless, once I moved back from the window, my foot on its edge, giving it one last thought

Once I put it from my mind—what it would be like to lean forward—to push on through

Though there were several points where we could have stopped it; though, later, this was the one that stood out to me most—me on the inside, my hands flipping the deadbolt, sliding the chain over—though I gave away the moment, Bean in first, whiskey on his breath, and the rest of them spilling in, the cat, too, with a big show of hissing and darting up the stairs

Though I will come back for the cat, later, after, though I will set out cans of tuna stolen from my mother's shelves, cartons of milk saved from school; though, in my head, I will name the cat Alley, though I will never see it again, will begin to question it existed, though Mandy will say she doesn't remember; though we made our way up the stairs, the flash-light now, along with the lighter, the crack of a beer popping open, my mouth on it

Though I showed them the ceiling, it already changed, less bright, only tin angels who didn't know how to dance; Mandy yawning, tipping back the bottle of wine, Rick shadowboxing in the corner, Jeffrey looking up with me, smiling, saying, It's something, his eyes already on the door

Though the stairway to the roof was dark, darker than the rest of the place, even, though Bean, in charge of the big flashlight, weaved and bobbed and twice had to be steadied from behind by Jeffrey and Rick, though no one fell down the stairs backward, no sound of skull against wood, which was what was making my heart all funny again, though no one fell, though no one was saying much, either, there in the dark, the second moment passing; though I was last to the roof's door, easier to open than I'd thought it would be, the others pushing it up and up, open to the cooling-off night without me

Apart from the wind, rushing at my face, then neck, then the rest of me, standing on the rooftop, the others already running side to side, Rick doing a cartwheel, Mandy saying, Look at this, oh my God, look

Apart from my feet, which soaked up warmth from the roof tiles, making me sweat, even now with the stars out, apart from the big machine or vent or something in the middle of the roof, apart from a few old metal signs, *Welcome to the Hilltop, The Best View in West Texas*, apart from the nothingness, the wide expanse of red-brown tile, tar or something else dark and sticky, bubbling up here and there where the tiles were missing, apart from the egg, Mandy throwing it across, east to west, it landing at the western edge, cracking but not frying, of course

Apart from Bean running over to check, Bean on his hands and knees, waiting for the egg to fry, Bean looking up, right at me, smiling a creepy smile, leaving his eyes out of it; apart from Bean saying, The edges are bubbling up, and It's happening; apart from no one buying it

Except for Rick, who left his boom box blaring an old-timey country song, who ran over, his feet clattering on the tile, his

light brown hair in a bowl cut we made fun of, that hair bouncing out from his head, flopping down, except for Rick with
his round Anishinaabe face, almost identical to Jeffrey's, dark
but still freckled, that face leaning down, Jeffrey and I looking
at each other, laughing already, Mandy twirling in the corner
by herself, the egg forgotten as soon as it was thrown

Except for Bean beckoning Rick closer, except for how I
should have been looking closer at Bean—Bean's baggy-ass-
pants, his pocket—at everything, really; except for Rick's
face, inches from the ground, Bean's hand lingering casually
behind Rick's head, then coming down; except for the egg,
gooey and yellow and on Rick's face now, of course; except
for everyone laughing

From this time, fast and faster, everything speeding up yet
slowing down somehow, more smoking and drinking, from
this time, Bean dancing fast by himself, something that could
have been traditional, then two-stepping with Rick, who'd
wiped his face on Bean's sleeve, where the egg crusted and
stuck, Bean dancing with Mandy last, her hair so tangled
now it was starting to clump, Bean saying to her, You're staying—you are

From this time, the wind everywhere, not at all died down
like it usually was at night, not going to bed like it should;
from this time, stars above, city lights below, if you could call
Holcomb a city, the lights of six thousand people blinking
and nodding; from this time, the lights blurring and circling,
all those circles, blue and yellow and red; from this time,
the music, old country about a man losing his wife, about
hard drinking, the music turned up loud, too loud, the music

moving slow in the back of my mind, always with the circle
lights, from this time

How liquor had always been hard to come by, beer, too, how
we all knew about being stoned, how that was cheap, easy,
how none of us drank, really, how hard we were hit, how
Bean drank the most, how the big whiskey bottle looked even
bigger in his hands, how Mandy and I looked at each other
across the roof, how we didn't dance together, how we were
both watching each other, just the same, and Bean, how he
was watching us back

How the downtown lights winked off around us, quiet settling over Main Street, how we didn't notice, didn't notice we
were the last ones, the ones with loud music and a spotlight
until there was a car below, two men in uniforms slamming
their doors, how there was a brighter light beamed up at us,
flashing lights below, how there were big feet now on the fire
escape, big feet in black, regulation shoes, climbing

Not including the time I stole two comic books, not including the time Bean and Rick got jumped walking home from
school, not including the time Roy and Mom got into a shoving match on the front lawn, not including the time Jeffrey's
dad blew up the water tower, not including the time some
guy tried to get Mandy into his car, this was the first time,
not including

Since Jeffrey and I were the oldest, since Mandy had passed
out in the corner, her hair covering her face, since Rick was
standing behind Jeffrey, cowering, really, since Jeffrey and I

were facing the stairs, listening, stuck for a moment, since we were not paying attention to Bean, since I, in particular, was not thinking of Bean

Since Jeffrey and I thought of the liquor at the same time, came unfrozen, willing our brains to work, our feet to move, gathering up the bottles and cans, the box long since blown away, both of us at the same time thinking of the big, empty vent in the middle of the roof, moving toward it, once, twice, hurrying, bottle after can after bottle down the shaft

Since the cops were on the roof, saying, Stop, and Put your hands up, and, On the ground, on the ground; since it was a lot to do all at once—the stopping, the hands, the ground—since there was so much all at once, since Bean was behind us by the western edge, Jeffrey and Rick facedown behind me, since I was on the ground, my head not quite down, since I turned in Bean's direction, since I could see but could not stop him—Bean who was not putting his hands over his head or dropping to the ground, who was moving forward along the edge

Since Bean had his arms together out in front; since Bean had brought Roy's gun

As soon as I saw—Bean, I yelled—as soon as I half rose, got as far as one knee, as soon as the cops saw Bean, their arms up in front, now, too, as soon as the new noise came, shots beside me, heading for Bean, as soon as I said, No, which is what they say in the movies, too, slow motion and loud, which is how I said it

As soon as I turned, Bean no longer there, then the sounds, below, *crash, smash, bam*, like in those comic books I stole that time, only without the bright, cool colors

As soon as we were up, running with the cops to the edge, as soon as Bean was below, in a clump of manzanita bushes; as soon as I thought of that time camping, how we'd gone hiking at Palo Duro Canyon, where all those Indians had had their horses killed, run off a cliff by the Texas Rangers; how Bean and I had gotten off the trail, how the manzanitas had reached out with their spindly branches, how they'd left scratches on the backs of our arms and legs

As soon as I told myself to focus, as soon as the big cop said, Holy shit; as soon as I was at the fire escape, climbing down, thinking about Bean's arms and legs, how they were going to itch—all I would let myself think—trying not to think about what was happening; trying not to think about those horses

Not including when I was born, not including when Bean broke his arm in the first grade; not including these lights and sirens, different from the first ones, the ride in the back of the ambulance bumpy and fast, the guys taking the corners so fast, Bean on a stretcher, me allowed in beside him, Bean's eyes closed, his body twisted to the left, off, his right leg with the bone sticking out; not including the millions of scratches

Not including just before, back at the hotel, by the bushes, how the paramedics had had to cut away part of his clothes to get him out, not including how they kept saying, Man, he's lucky; not including his breath, coming out ragged but regular, coming out, anyhow; not including the paramedics' hands on him, one of them saying, No, no gunshot wound; not including the small cop, just out of high school, it looked like, how he kept saying, Thank you, Jesus, thank you; not

including how he was crying, right there next to the manzanitas, not including how he was down on his knees right
there by the Hilltop

Not including the arrival, the hospital hallway bright white,
the pee smell just another thing making me sick, not including
Mom, who should have been wailing, who was quiet, so quiet;
not including Mom pacing the halls dead quiet

Not including the surgery, the pressure on Bean's brain, not
including Mom's eyes on me, worse than Bean's had been, not
including Jeffrey and Rick and Mandy and their parents, who
all hugged me, which made me feel how bad this was, made
me feel it in my spine and hands and ankles; not including the
TV in the waiting area blaring *Wheel of Fortune*, not including
the cold, hard, plastic seats; not including the waiting

After Bean did not die but also did not get better, after
learning about the Glasgow Coma Scale, after Bean opened
his eyes twice briefly, after he never really woke up but was
not considered brain dead

After I finished high school, after Jeffrey left, after Rick and
I started working construction, after Mandy and I went out,
broke up, got engaged, broke up, got married

After Benjamin was born, after we debated whether to call
him Bean, for his uncle, after we settled on Ben, which was
close but not unlucky; after I stopped jumping at every siren;
after dinner every Wednesday, visiting Bean, after bringing
him cookies or bread Mandy made, knowing the nurses gave
it to the other patients but bringing it, just the same

After seeing Mom in the hallway this Wednesday, spring
again, ash on her forehead from church; after the way she
looked at Ben with something so close to hope but not quite

making it, after I said, No, sorry, we're going camping for Easter

After we told each other with our eyes that we were still so very sorry

If we had been white kids, Mom said, if the good citizens of Holcomb would have torn down the Hilltop, if the Holcombs had all died out, if the city hadn't declared the building historic

If Rick and I hadn't worked construction, if we hadn't been flat broke, if the hotel restoration hadn't been the only job going

If the roof hadn't looked damn near the same, if my legs hadn't shook so bad on the way up, Rick behind me, saying, Lunchtime, man

If I hadn't clocked out early, picked up Mandy and Ben, heading for Palo Duro early—Beating the crowd, I said—if Mandy hadn't nodded okay, knowing the truth and packing anyway, already telling Ben about the canyon, the horses

If we had arrived earlier, a little more of daylight left, if there had been extra batteries for the flashlight

If the dark hadn't come on like it always does, like it has a right to, if Mandy and Ben hadn't been snoring behind me in the tent

If I could stop sitting here, outside the tent, if I could stop being so very far outside; if I could stop seeing those circles, eyes open or closed, if those circles could stop being so bright

If I could tell this story right; if I could stop telling it

Conjunctions

For a third grade teacher, Ben told her, you sure do cuss a lot.
His hand shook as he said it, making the chalk against the board
wiggle. He wanted to drop the chalk again—he liked the way
it felt when it slipped between his fingers, the way the wall felt
cool against the top of his head when he bent to pick up the
chalk. He wanted to drop it for the fourteenth time, to keep
counting and feeling the coolness, despite how the back of his
neck was pinking up, how he could feel the gasps and whispers
of the fourteen other students behind Ms. Winston.

Most of all, though, Ben wanted to tell Ms. Winston to stop,
just stop. Cursing, even under-the-breath cursing had always
made him cry, and didn't she know he could not afford to cry
in class again this week? Didn't she know it was hard enough
being five years old and in the third grade and at a new school
without everybody calling you Big Baby Ben or Crybaby Ben
or Ben, the Indian Blubber Boy?

My vocabulary is not the issue here, Ben, Ms. Winston said. If you don't know how to conjugate the verb, please sit down.

Miscreant, he thought. Old fleabag. He could feel the tears starting up, his color rising, and he turned his face to the side, to the open window, and he felt the breeze bring the color down, some. He was pale for an Indian, even for a mixed-blood, even for a Rampert. He was pale and knew too many words, and knowing them never helped, anyway.

The windows were the crank kind, the childproof kind that only opened half way. But they were made to hold in larger boys, and Ben was small, even for his age. He had done it before. Two weeks ago, when Tommy Frederickson was vomiting in the far corner, Ben had pulled himself up to the small, brick ledge, shimmied his legs through the opening and made the rest of himself limp as he slipped through. That was the key, the going limp part, and doing something sort of like the wave with the arms and hands so that they followed the body in a natural motion.

I could do it, he thought. I could show these morons. To show, he thought. Will show. Showed. Have shown. And then he was hurtling himself at Ms. Winston's podium, and it was falling, her glasses and coffee cup clattering, papers skittering. And then Ben was doing it. He was at the window, was making himself small and limp, his arms waving first, and then the rest of him shimmying, too, the rest of him out.

The gas station was just down the street, the bus stop two blocks further, but both lay across the street from the school. Ben had run the block and a half to the stoplight, and he jogged back and forth while he waited for the light to turn, the broken piece of chalk still cool and nice in his right fist. He had been trying not to look behind him or side to side—to focus, will focus, have focused—but it was hard not to look around. The man standing next to him smelled bad and kept lurching down at him, saying, Hey, man, you got a light? And though Ben shook his head, the man seemed not to notice or understand.

The light turned; it was the kind with numbers that counted down, and Ben counted along with them: 30, 29, 28, 27. Everyone around him hurried, their legs so much longer, and Ben broke into a half-trot that wasn't a run, exactly, but that allowed him to keep pace with the last of the people. It seemed important not to run, not to stand out in that way, but it seemed important, too, not to be last. The light was flashing the number four by the time Ben made it to the other side, by the time he trotted past a fast-moving old lady with a walker. The yellow hand came on under the numbers as Ben passed the walker, as he moved up the curb to the gas station and through the pinging door.

The tall man with the dark hair leaned behind the counter. Ben nodded to him, and the tall man nodded back. He had a paper spread out in front of him, want ads, and he had circled four in bright red ink. Ben stood there a moment, still in the doorway, staring at the circles. His mom had done that with the Dallas-Forth Worth paper when they were still back at home in Holcomb. She'd circled apartments and jobs, but she and his father had not been able to agree on a circle. They'd moved twice already in their first month in Fort Worth. The first apartment had been close to his first school, which was supposed to be one of the best in the state, but then his test scores had come back, and there had been this new school, one with older kids and mean Ms. Winston and his mom and dad now all the way across the city, making more circles in another newspaper.

In the meantime, Ben was stuck with the new streetlights and cars, with the old motel behind the school that was called a dormitory but wasn't, really, with his ball glove underneath the bed they said was his. All because of his stupid, special brain.

Ben rubbed his eyes and looked back, but the circles were still there. He backed out the door slowly, and the tall man behind the counter nodded again, gave him a little *hey, man* salute. Across the street at the school, a black-and-white car loitered, Ms. Winston and the principal next to it.

The city bus huffed and shuddered to its stop by the store, and Ben's fist tightened around his chalk. To run. Will run. Have run. Ran.

The window on the city bus was cool, and Ben leaned his face against it, willing his breathing to slow, to normalize. That's all he wanted, really. For no one to swear. For everything to go back to normal. He had one quarter left over from the change in his sock, and he palmed it in his left hand, the chalk still in his right.

He was riding all the way across town, something he had never done before by himself, and he tried not to think about that. He felt the coolness of the quarter against his skin and tried to concentrate on that feeling instead. He remembered the first time his mother had given him a quarter, how she'd flipped it in the air, how she'd said, Don't spend it all in one place. How he'd known, even then, what twenty-five times twenty-five was, how he was multiplying in his head, liking the way that felt, liking the quarter's smoothness, too, its cool weight against his skin.

His first night at the Hotel for Tiny Geniuses, Ben had tried to keep a positive outlook. That's what his mother had said to him over and over on the ride there, and so he tried not to think of her physically—the way her hair smelled, the little pat she gave his covers when she tucked him in—but only of her words. To survive, Ben knew, his family would have to become an abstraction.

The hotel hadn't been a hotel for years, had been a half-way house in between, and was now a strange, squat dormitory. It was a barracks-style affair, a long-stay type hotel for the poor or for those who wanted to hide. It was just like the place outside Holcomb, Ben thought, that place he and his parents had stayed in that time when his father had quit his job, when they had to move in the middle of the night but were still pretending everything was fine. That's what Ben associated with cinder block walls—pretending—and so when he arrived at the hotel, he set about doing just that, forcing himself to look up at the bigger boys, forcing his round face into a smile.

Which was a giant mistake, of course. To humiliate. Will humiliate. Have humiliated. Have Ben humiliated.

Tommy Frederickson was the tallest, blondest kid at the hotel. He was the smartest in math and science, in part, because the other kids all were afraid to challenge his answers, in part because he was, of course, the school bully. Ben recognized him instantly—there had been one back in Holcomb (Lyle

Anders) and one at the last school (Joe Bass), and each time, the bigger boy seemed to have thought of new, worse ways to torment Ben before he'd even arrived.

Ben had been at the hotel about twenty minutes, was still fingering his new nametag and situating his ball glove under the bottom bunk when Tommy and two of his friends appeared behind him, standing beside his bed. He'd taken the lower bunk, of course, because of his height. Because he hadn't wanted to cause any trouble. Ben, the bed-wetter, Tommy said. Don't you know only bed-wetters take the bottom bunk?

And then the front of his jeans were wet, the boys having pulled their water bottles from behind their backs collectively, and Ben's new roommate was lingering there in the doorway, then backing away with his eyes on the floor, quiet, which is how Ben tried to be, too, from there forward. To yield. Will yield. Have yielded. Stop.

It took a long time for the bus to go across the city, to reach the right corner, which was near his house, his mother and father. But Ben knew he couldn't go there, knew the black-and-white car would be looking. Instead, when the bus finally stopped, Ben stumbled his way down the steps, his left foot asleep, both legs needing a good stretch. His fingertips touched the rough metal of the stairs, and he lingered there a moment, balancing, before the crowd swept him out, onto the street, the chalk sticky and warm in his hand.

The bus stop sat on the right side of the street, so there was no counting, no need, this time, to think about running. This time, he turned right and took his time, counting the steps from the bus stop, across the cement sidewalk, then the cool, long, grass, up to the big, brick building, the row of window on window.

He found the one he was looking for easily enough. Ms. Hansen stood at the front of the class, her blond hair swept up neatly just like he remembered. It had been less than a month, of course, but it seemed like so much longer. The class was going over the alphabet, and Stephanie Meeks was at the board, practicing her *C*s.

Ben raised his hand to the window, but everyone was looking forward. He stood on his tiptoes and pressed his forehead against the cool glass, still keeping one hand up, hopeful. Stephanie was finishing her *C*s, moving on to the *D*s, and though no one turned around and no one waved, Ben kept his hand up. He could hear, in the distance, what sounded like the wail of the black-and-white car. He could feel the coolness of the window against his forehead, his tears threatening once again. He tried to focus on Stephanie, the straight backs of her *D*s, their measured, even curves, and on Ms. Hansen whose precise hair nodded encouragement as Stephanie wrote.

But the sirens came on, growing louder. To fall. Will fall. Fell. Have fallen. He pressed himself harder against the window. And then the words were there for Ben, loud against the pressure of the sirens, and the chalk was there, too, warmer than it had been, but still there, still held tight in his waving hand. He moved it against the glass, his breath more even, more deliberate with each letter—to hold, will hold, held, have held on, will hold on.

Killing Elvis

Ditches wide and dark all around, fog thick enough for a hundred spoons, and my friend Jeffrey watches a blackbird who is not watching him back. Technically, Jeffrey is not my friend, is instead my husband, and the bird, though it is black, may not be a blackbird. Jeffrey is the one who knows about birds, who can call them what they are, but he's leaning over this one and its broken beak, and he's crying. I want to know if it's a blackbird, raven, or crow, and how I might know the difference, but Jeffrey is stomping around the ditch, his dark hair flying, and *Raven or crow?* seems like the wrong question.

Jeffrey was my biology lab instructor six years ago, back in college, and we've been together since. I've seen him yell, have heard him curse in Anishinaabemowin and English, but this is the first time I've seen him cry. To say it's a spectacle would be making it small. He's kicking the sides of the ditch. He's holding his round face in his hands, shaking it side to side, stretching the freckles. His breath comes in hiccups, and his shoulders shake in time with the idling of our pickup but out of sync with Elvis who is still on the radio, singing about wise men, fools, love.

Jeffrey is yelling, I hate you, and I am glad it is not quite seven a.m., that the two-lane is empty of all but us and the bird we've hit. If no one sees this, does it happen? My mother's voice says, *No, of course not. Close your eyes,* but I don't. The Bitterroot Mountains hover beyond, the big darkness that is Montana all around. I know Elk Mountain stands to the north with Mt. Snowy to the west and Lookout Pass to the south.

My vote is to go east, to drive as fast as we can until the prairie opens up and short grass tickles my ankles and I can take a deep, full, Minnesota breath. Montana is dangerous. We are fresh out of a tent and our honeymoon, and I'm standing in front of the truck, trying to decide whether to put my hand on Jeffrey's shoulder or to step back into the cab and quietly close the door when Jeffrey stops spinning and kicking and kneels over the bird. I move in behind him, the dew from the tall grass on my pant legs. I wrap my arms around his waist and lean in.

I could cut it open, I say. I could tell you what he had for a last meal.

I want Jeffrey to laugh, to close his eyes and forget where we've just been. His father lives ten miles back down the two-lane in a town called Thompson Falls. Before this trip, Jeffrey hadn't tried to see his father in nine years, since the last time his father got out of prison.

Jeffrey sits down in the ditch next to the bird, and I sit next to him. Nothing in our eight days of marriage has prepared me for this, but I take his hands from his face anyway. I thread my fingers through his, feel the cool metal of his ring against skin. Wrappers from a gas station sandwich wrinkle and curl around our feet and knees. I kick away a Coke can and bend to kiss the underside of his wrists. The shaking has slowed so it's more like an occasional jerk or seizure.

Steak, I say. I'll bet he had a steak sandwich and a Coke.

Jeffrey takes his hands from mine and puts them back on his face. The grass is cold and damp through my jeans, and he topples over so his head is in my lap. The fog lifts some, and his face shines pale and spotted under the sun's first weak light.

Unlikely, he says.

I run my hand through his hair, feathering it back, knowing it will flip forward, back to how it was before I touched it. He doesn't like me to play with his hair, and his shoulders shift and squirm beneath me.

But possible, I say. I want to say, Crows are common. I want to say, Crows like this one are dying on highways across America at a rate of 3.2 per second. I want him to laugh. I move my fingers over the bridge of his nose, under his eyes, down toward the sides of his mouth, connecting the freckles—an old game—one he tolerates, one I think he sometimes enjoys. I want to say, Let's go home, to the city, to buildings and noise. I want to say, It could be worse, you know. I want to remind him that not everyone gets to have a father, even a hard-drinking, ex-con father, but the corners of his mouth are moving a little toward a smile, and the fog is lifting. Just enough so that where it was dark overhead, now there is the start of sun.

When people ask my Irish Catholic mother why she married my Blackfoot father, James Rampert, five times out of ten she'll say because he had nice teeth and looked like a cross between Burt Reynolds and Elvis. In particular, she blames those teeth: they were white and straight and seemed to reveal good character. The other five times she'll say one name—Clyde Sykes—then give a long, blue-eyed stare, punctuated only by a deep menthol drag and sigh.

My parents meet at a party outside Talbot, Minnesota, in a cornfield along the Blue Earth River. It's the end of summer, and Clyde Sykes is leaving for Vietnam the next day. He is one of the last to be called up. My mother's best friend loves Clyde Sykes, who is my father's best friend. It has been a good year for corn, plenty of rain, plenty of heat, and the dark green stalks of my grandfather's field twist and wave overhead, some reaching nearly ten feet tall.

My parents sit in the back of my father's Chevy pickup, the nearest seat to the keg. They have both just graduated high school, my mother in Talbot, my father a few miles north in Garden City. His family has been in Minnesota only a year, down from the Blood Reserve in Alberta, and my father is still nervous about the absence of mountains, all the missing pine trees. He squints into the corn, trying to make it taller, to make it something it's not, turning his eyes to slits, almost able to block out the flat land past the cornfield.

Hours into the party, somebody decides Clyde Sykes needs to have some money in his pocket for his journey. Clyde is only five feet four, has three older, six-feet-tall brothers, and so is good at jumping, at catching all manner of things in his mouth.

They start off easy, somebody lobbing a Frisbee up past the corn where it lingers amid stars before spiraling down. It finds its home easily between Clyde's teeth. My father takes off his baseball cap, and those who believe in Clyde, and those who are generous or drunk, throw in coins and small bills.

After the apple, which Clyde catches then eats without using his hands, but before the goldfish, my mother turns to my father and says, Are you like Clyde? My father is busy with the hat. When he doesn't respond, my mother drinks deep from her plastic cup, says, You know, Chippewa, like Clyde.

Eventually this word—Chippewa—which is given to them by their enemies, will fall out of favor, will become Ojibwe, which will coexist with Anishinaabe, their word for *original man* or *the people.* But now my father turns the hat round and round, and boys who would say they are men but are not yet throw in their coins, some landing soft, some glancing off the tailgate with a ping and thud. No, says my father, I'm not Chippewa. My mother drinks again, leans into him further. The corn waves and shimmers.

Somebody brings out the goldfish though no one will ever be able to remember who it was, where it came from. The goldfish is not gold at all but the color of flame. My father could lean into my mother now, could say, *Saa,* no, I'm not Chippewa, I'm Blackfoot, Kainai from Canada, from the Blood Reserve just north of Montana. But the goldfish is there, being pulled from its plastic bag, and everyone hoots and throws coins, and my father misses his chance.

The goldfish flame goes up, bright against the yelling and stars, and my father smiles, those teeth quick and bright. He leans in to kiss my mother, the fish falling through the dark to Clyde. Someone yells, Goddamn, he's going to catch it, and my parents' lips are meeting, and the goldfish flame lingers against the darkness, a trick of balance, and then it is going down and down, and they move together, my father's hands on my mother's hair, and then it is all quiet, all dark.

During the third night of biology lab, I am hunching over a frog, legs splayed and tacked. My lab partner, a blond boy whose name neither Jeffrey nor I will remember, is missing. Though I have, on my own, slit the frog belly to chin, I am unable to identify its parts, to quarter and label the heart as required. It is almost nine; all the other students have filed out, leaving Jeffrey, me, the frog, its pickled smell, and the hum of the fluorescent lights.

I am a music history major with an American Indian Studies minor, but biology is my favorite class this semester. Class starts with Jeffrey, Mr. Bairnd, lecturing, and then we move to dissection. It's the lecture I love, the way Jeffrey takes his time pronouncing the strange biology words—*microvilli*, *lysosome*, *capsid*. It's the way his hair needs cutting or growing, how its in-between length leaves it in constant need of brushing from his eyes or behind his ears.

My roommate is Anishinaabe, from the Mille Lac Reservation just north of the Twin Cities, the university. She works at the Indian Studies Center on campus where Jeffrey also works part-time. For twenty dollars and two history papers, she pulls Jeffrey's file, fills in the high school years for me.

I know a little already about Jeffrey's growing up years, from my cousin Grady down in Texas. They were friends back then, so I know Jeffrey's Anishinaabe but was born in Texas. From the file, I learn he spent high school in northern Montana, just south of the Blood Reserve, where my father and his family are from, where I still have cousins and uncles I've never met. Jeffrey and I are each other's opposite, I think; we should have been switched at birth. Of course, I will later revise this theory, but for now I am twenty-one, in awe of coincidence and possibility.

Jeffrey finishes putting away papers and tidying up the left-over bits of frogs from other stations. By the time he reaches my table, I've identified the heart, have it out between the kidneys, the spools that he says are intestines.

They look like brains, I say.

Jeffrey laughs, taps the frog's head, which is pinned down but otherwise intact. *Niinimoshenh*, he says, I think his brain might be in there.

Later, after class, I will run back to the apartment, repeating the sounds of *niinimoshenh* to myself over and over, imagining how they might be spelled out. I will pull my roommate's Anishinaabemowin/English dictionary from the top shelf, will learn *niinimoshenh* means *my sweetheart*.

But I am in love even before I know this, with the softness of his voice, his hair falling into his eyes, his large hands that move so delicately as they take the heart and slice it into fours.

When Jeffrey is seven, his father, Wade, takes him fishing at Whitefish Lake, a half hour north of Kalispell, where they live. Rick, Jeffrey's brother, who is five, has wet the bed the night before and so is made to stay home. Each time this story is told, Jeffrey says this trip, its pieces, are earned, deserved, and I say, *You were seven*, but he won't hear it.

The night before the trip, with both his parents long since asleep in the apartment's one bedroom, Jeffrey and Rick lie awake on the pullout couch in the living room, too excited for sleep, kicking each other under the covers. Jeffrey tells Rick scary stories, which make him breathless, and Jeffrey makes sure Rick's water glass is refilled each time it empties.

When Wade rouses them at dawn, he finds Rick shivering, wet and cold, his side of the bed clammy and rank. Jeffrey is curled up in the far corner of the bed, dry.

The half hour to Whitefish Lake passes quickly, Jeffrey sitting up straight and tall in the pickup's cab, eating the third donut as fast as he can, licking his fingers but not enjoying it, his stomach snarled with shame. Flathead Lake is closer to Kalispell and is bigger, but Whitefish is where Wade had gone fishing with his own father.

We're going to catch so many goddamned fish, Wade says. We're not going to know what to do with them all.

The lake is empty except for a few old men in saggy hats on the far side, and there are fish—brown trout, carp, a bullhead with eyes so big Jeffrey almost drops him.

Steady there, boy, Wade says, laughing. His hands guide the fish off the hook and into the net, and he and Jeffrey stand over it, watching it flop and writhe.

Though there are no pictures from that day, I can picture how it was—pine trees all around, the sun warming their round faces, the identical freckles, their hair, black and red, standing up in the back and at the crown. This is where I like the story to end or maybe just before this, at the moment of the catch. Before Wade steers Jeffrey close to the fish, the father's hands on the son's shoulders, the weight of the father large behind the son. The son wanting to turn his head away but also wanting to watch. And they do, together, as the fish gasps for breath.

And the story doesn't end there, either. Wade has tied a six pack to another line, the line to a nearby rock, and by noon, the beer is pulled from the water, good and cold, and he offers one to Jeffrey, who says later that the first drink wasn't at all like orange soda but was good just the same.

It is almost dark by the time they make their way around the shoreline to the truck. In less than a year, the truck will be gone, repossessed, driven off while Wade screams and throws lawn chairs, but for now, it waits, just around the last curve of water.

Wade walks ahead, the big net dangling, bouncing against his long, thin legs. Jeffrey carries the smaller net, which had been fine and light in the morning but now weighs against him. The fish slap his legs, and their smell—dank and clammy—makes him think of Rick, the bed, and Jeffrey turns his head away from the smell to the lake. But it is hard to see what's ahead, and there's a hole, wider than he is by an inch or so and a few inches deeper than he is tall. It catches him mid-stride. His left leg slips in first, his right sliding in after it so fast he barely has time to let go of the net, to catch himself with his elbows. His breath goes down the hole with him. Once it comes back, the sun is sinking into the lake, and his father stands over him, holding both nets, his expression made larger by the light from his cigarette.

Posthole, Wade says. Must have been a big-ass sign there.

Wade leans in close, so close Jeffrey can smell his sweat and breath, and the nausea rolls in again. He turns his head and bites his lip. He closes his eyes. He would not cry. When he opens them, the cigarette has been snubbed out a few inches from the hole, and Wade's back is closer to the truck, a net slung over each shoulder, bouncing against his sides.

You're going to miss the best part, Wade says. He says it loud, calling it over his shoulder with a little wave.

Jeffrey won't tell the rest of this story; for him, it ends there, in the hole, the bad smells closing in. I've had to piece it together with bits from Rick and Melissa, their mother, who doesn't like to tell it either but will after a tall bottle of Thanksgiving wine.

Wade leaves the lake for his own father's house, the fish at his sides, night coming on through the trees. He turns the pickup off a half-block shy of the house he grew up in and coasts, lights off. The house is empty, and I've always wondered if this pleased or disturbed him—if he wanted an audience. The last of the catch still flops and twitches, and Wade waits in the cab till that stops, till the dark takes a permanent hold.

The rest we know from the yearly Christmas card. How Wade's parents come home from the grocery store to the fish—in the petunia beds, in between the screen and storm doors, lined up as a border between the yard and road. It takes two days for them to find the bullhead in the mailbox.

But this has never been the part of the story I want to know. I want to know what Jeffrey does when his father returns. Does he take his father's hand the first time it's offered? Does Jeffrey cry or yell or go quiet when his father lifts him up, out of that

hole? Do his legs kick or have they gone limp, saving the fight
for later? I want to know about the ride home—Jeffrey sitting
lower in his seat or slumped against the door, his head resting
against the window's cool glass. I know the result, though, if
not the details. How he won't see scary movies. How he won't
retell the scary stories I tell him. How he leaves his students
alone in the lab for hours on the day the fish come out to be
taken apart.

DAY SEVEN

The only room left in the only hotel in Thompson Falls has a
bed that sags in the middle, and in front of the television, the
carpet is stained so dark it's easy to imagine an animal sacrifice.
Jeffrey is in the shower, water beating against the faux glass
door, and steam seeps from the bathroom into the main room
where I sit on the bed. We have been married seven days. This
will be our first married night in a bed, such as it is.

The TV has four channels that show two infomercials, a
repeat of the evening news, and the last of the late-night movies, one of those with Clint Eastwood and an ape? orangutan?
monkey? In a few short hours, it will be morning. In a few short
hours, I'll be meeting my father in law. I choose the movie
and sink back into the pillows, tiredness moving over me in
a sharp, tall wave. I think about how close we are to Canada,
to the Blood Reserve, to family I've never seen. I think about
Jeffrey and me at the border, but I can't imagine it without
seeing my mother there, her tears loud and hot, steam rising
from her that makes us both sweat.

I don't know how long I sleep before Jeffrey leaves the
shower for the bed, before he stands over me in a towel, shaking his wet hair in my face. I startle awake and reach for him,

smiling, but he steps back. Clint Eastwood and the monkey/ape trade blows with two men in wide-lapelled suits. My smile sinks, and I feel tears forming. I am thinking of words like *newlywed, honeymoon, love*. I am just about to cry when Jeffrey leans forward, when he takes my hand and pulls me up to him, in front of the television where Eastwood and the orangutan now drive the getaway car.

Dance with me, he says. He pulls me into him, his hands on my hands, and I expect his towel to fall, to cover the animal sacrifice stain beneath us, but he's knotted the corners tight.

Niinimoshenh, he says, *niinzaagi'giin. Zaagi* is love, but *zagakin* is *to tidy, to put away*. I lean close to be sure which he is saying, but there is only the sound of tires squealing as Clint and the ape round the last curve, as the screen blares *every which way you can*, as the names of the actors tumble down it.

DAY ONE

Jeffrey and I have been going to see a therapist in Minneapolis, where we live, for over a year. For the last few months, the therapist has been saying maybe Montana isn't the best idea for a honeymoon. Too much history. He and I agree the South is nice in August. We agree on the Smoky Mountains, on being at Graceland for my birthday, for Elvis' death day. Jeffrey nods along like he agrees, too, and after our courthouse ceremony, we head southwest out of the Twin Cities on Highway 169 as planned. I am asleep within an hour, and at St. Peter, a town stripped of trees by a tornado, Jeffrey stops going south. We pause once for gas in eastern South Dakota, and I wonder if things would have been different if I had fully come out of sleep then, if there would have been time to turn back.

Instead, I stretch and yawn and reach for the door handle on the second stop in northwestern South Dakota, in a little town called Faith that borders the Cheyenne River Reservation—Montana less than three hours away. I'm still thinking we're on our way to Graceland, are about half-way there, so I'm imagining the green hills and tall oaks of Missouri, but no matter how hard I rub my eyes, this place is flat and brown with tall grass that waves like wheat in the empty lot next to the station. Jeffrey stands beside the truck, the gas humming into the tank in its steady, familiar rhythm. He has the window squeegee and a paper towel in his hands. The sky is threatening a storm, is the same yellow-brown as the ground, so it looks like Jeffrey has been painted into a backdrop.

I packed your sweaters, he says. And some thick socks. It gets cold in the mountains, he says, even in the summer. He is trying to smile as he says it. He is not quite looking at me.

We had agreed to leave our cell phones back in the apartment. Out of touch, romantic. The only payphone in evidence leans next to the abandoned lot, and there is no phone at the end of the dangling cord, and besides, who would I call? My mother would ask if I remembered to pack the bourbon. She would say, Then, you'd have a little piece of the South to keep you warm. She would say, South Dakota? Watch out for the Indians, and then she would laugh. Jeffrey and I have been married less than twenty-four hours. The scrub flattens out, brown and endless, and I close my eyes, know I will keep seeing it.

When Jeffrey is nine, his father works small construction jobs around Kalispell, putting up drywall, sanding floors—finishing work, mostly. It is his dream to have his own business, to start a project from the beginning and see it through. It is late August when Wade's friend Relly helps him get on the crew for a strip mall on the south side of town. School has just started, and when Jeffrey tells this story, he says everything felt new.

Relly lives down the street from Jeffrey's apartment building in a house he owns outright. He picks Wade up every morning at six, honking the horn out in front of the building.

He thinks he's too good for knocking on our door, Wade says, too good to hike his ass up three flights of stairs.

Jeffrey and his brother sleep on the foldout couch in the living room just a few feet from the kitchen where Wade waits for the honk of the horn. He is ready early, pacing back and forth on the linoleum, gripping his thermos and lunch pail, stopping every few steps to kick the low cabinet doors, which never stay shut. Rick sleeps until their mother wakes them for school, but Jeffrey squints toward the kitchen, watches his father stiffen, hears him kick the loudest each time Relly honks the horn.

They've been on the job two weeks the night Wade doesn't come home. Jeffrey's mother has made spaghetti, and the three of them sit at the table until well past dark, watching the grease on top of the sauce come together and split apart. Rick reaches for the noodles, but Melissa slaps his hand.

No, she says. We wait.

It's almost dawn when Jeffrey awakens, a rough hand over his mouth, the other catching his arm, pulling him past Rick, carrying him down the three flights of stairs. Wade's breath smells sour, and he doesn't move his hand from Jeffrey's mouth until they're seated in the cab of Relly's truck.

There's a job, Wade says. I need to know if you're up for it. Jeffrey's bare feet hang down off the seat, banging against the sides of the gas can. He nods to his father. He squares his shoulders and resists the urge to rub his eyes. Sure, he says. Okay.

Kitchen lights warm the back of Relly's house as they pass. The front of the house is dark, and something looks different in the front yard, but Jeffrey can't quite place it. He says he half-expected them to pause, to honk the horn, but half of him knew they wouldn't. Wade holds the bottle between his legs. He raises it to the kitchen lights in a mock toast and then drinks big, some of the liquid escaping down his chin. Jeffrey turns his face away from his father's and looks through the back window toward the lights.

Jeffrey stays turned around, watching house after house fall away, until the spaces between the houses grow longer, until the houses give way to empty lots with large white signs announcing the coming of Shady Hills, Oak Centre, Willow Way. The construction site stands empty, beams rising up bare against the pre-dawn light. Everything is turning—it is that time of year—and the hoarfrost grass under Jeffrey's feet numbs his toes first, and then the cold works its way up. He wears a Denver Broncos sweatshirt and a pair of Rick's navy sweatpants, the elastic too tight and riding up his calves, digging in. His sweatpants had all been in the wash, and that's what he thinks as his father takes the tree limbs from the back of the truck and begins piling them in the center of the beams—how his mother should have done the laundry sooner, how then he wouldn't be cold.

Jeffrey, Wade says. Bring that on over.

The gas can is nearly as big as he is, and the lid isn't as tight as it could be, so some sloshes out onto him, the smell strong but familiar.

Careful, Wade says. We don't want to waste it. He takes the gas from Jeffrey and begins pouring it onto the limbs, the beams.

Jeffrey heads toward the pickup, but his father grabs his arm, turning him the other way.

Get out on the road now.

Wade pulls the truck up to the center of the beams, and for a moment, it looks like the first customer has arrived early. Jeffrey stands on the road, feeling the gasoline on his feet, his shins, how it's drying his skin, pulling it tight. Later, he will say it was hard to stay there on the road. Part of him wanted to run to his father, to pull his arm, to say, *please*; another part of him wanted to run for home, of course, but it's the rest of himself that scares him still—how he wanted to be covered in gasoline, how his legs wanted to move toward the fire. Now his father turns to him. Wade is slipping off his thin T-shirt, ripping it into strips, and then the strips are on fire, and then the brush, the beams, the cab they had just been sitting in.

We built that, Wade says. It's ours. He puts a bare arm around Jeffrey's shoulders, and Jeffrey can feel the muscles and bone. Jeffrey can't look at me when he tells this part of the story—how Wade pulls on his arm, how Jeffrey holds himself as still as he can, resisting his father but trying also to resist the more powerful urge, the one to walk steady and fast, straight into the fire. But Wade is stronger, and for once, his strength is good, and he pulls Jeffrey toward town, away from the popping and hissing of wood catching flame. They stop a few yards down the road, and Wade turns Jeffrey around for a last glance.

We built that, Wade says. We built that, and we can take it down.

Jeffrey closes his eyes, and it is then that he can picture it—what is wrong with Relly's yard, the tall tree out front. It's off balance, its lower limbs missing, not like they've been trimmed back but like they've been severed. It's top-heavy now, the top limbs thick with dark birds that move up and up, climbing.

Just ten weeks remain before my birth. My mother's belly stretches so far that she can only imagine her feet, and this lack of clarity bothers her. She hasn't had a cigarette in five months, three weeks, and two days. Summer is starting up in Talbot, and the men are in the fields, doing the last of the planting. It has rained all of the last sixteen days when my mother picks up the phone, when she orders the tickets in a voice pulled tight by its need for distraction.

The tickets arrive the first week of June. The concert is June 24th in Madison, Wisconsin, a five-hour drive from Talbot. Not too far, my mother thinks. Possible.

She makes my father his favorite meal—pot roast with carrots and potatoes, fry bread steaming and glistening on the side of the plate. After dinner, the plates pushed back, the coffee before them, my mother brings the tickets out from the pocket in her skirt. She leaves them there a minute—under the table, under the curve of her belly—before pulling them out, placing them before my father.

In the version of this story I like best, my father says, *Elvis? Hell, yes.* He is pleased at my mother's secret. He doesn't ask where the money came from; the muscles along the side of his jaw do not begin to twitch.

In this version, my parents drive the Chevy to Madison for what will end up being one of Elvis' last shows. Elvis will wear his Mexican sundial suit; he will close the concert with Can't Help Falling in Love. My father will sing it to my mother in the truck on the way home, his white teeth making her remember. In this version, my birth and Elvis' death are a bittersweet coincidence, the sweet lingering like a song.

My mother tells this version when she's happy and when I'm not, when she knows I need to hear it. The other version comes out like an old uncle for dried-out Sunday dinners, for small holidays. In this version, my father says, *Elvis tickets?* and *Where did the money come from?* and *Kitóho, saa; you heard me, no.*

This version ends with the plates on the floor, some of them chipped beyond repair, my father having stormed out long ago, my mother sitting in the kitchen, her bare feet propped up on the table so she can see them. She vows then that no child of hers will ever step foot on any reservation or reserve, that no child of hers will be raised Indian. This is a vow she will keep, regret, then keep again. She wiggles her toes, counting them, before she lights the match and puts it to the cigarette. Before she closes her eyes.

This version ends with my birth as the pinnacle of bad timing. *It was his fault*, my mother says, *all your father's fault.* In this version, my father is responsible for killing Elvis.

THE DAY BEFORE

My mother and I sit at my kitchen table. Suitcases lie open on the couch, some half-filled, some still empty. Jeffrey is at the university giving a lecture, and rain is gathering outside. I don't know why I want this story, but I do—I want the best version—the one where my parents see Elvis. The one that ends with them in the car on the way back from the concert, my father steering with one hand, the other on my mother's knee. I want the version where Elvis' death is a giant conspiracy. I want the version where luck wins.

Tell it, I say. Come on, Mom, you know you want to.

My mother looks at me across the wide expanse of table. She lights a cigarette. She gives me version number three. Katherine Anne, she says, I have no idea where you get such ideas. I never bought any Elvis tickets. I don't even like Elvis.

I go to the courthouse the next day wanting a fourth version, the one my father would have told, the one without the constants of the first three—Elvis dead before the summer ends, my father dead before I am born, dead before Elvis, surprised by a Buick as he walks to the grocery store one morning for milk.

It is hard to know how he would tell this story, but I like to think version number four is full of fast, good turns—that it's the kind to leave you laughing, wanting more. That it's the kind to continue.

DAY EIGHT

Wade's house sits at the corner of Thompson Falls Road and Fourth Street. It is just past six a.m., and Jeffrey and I sit in our truck in front of the house, looking over its front porch, which sags like the hotel bed. It's still dark out, not quite dawn, and is foggy, too, so we leave the lights dim. Even from the truck, I can see we're too late, but just barely. A half dozen garbage bags line the curb, and the lawn shows the zigs and zags of a recent mow, but inside the house, the plastic mini-blinds hang in tatters, and beyond them, through the front window, I can see the house is empty. The sign out front reads *For Rent*.

We have just missed him, and something like relief rushes through me, but it's not pure, is mixed with a loss so big it surprises me. I lay my head on the dash and close my eyes, and when I open them, Jeffrey is out of the truck, and his door is making that ping, ping sound that happens when you leave things open wide.

Jeffrey is in the middle of the yard, leaning on the sign, alternately pushing and pulling it with both hands. The sun soon will move into its place in the sky. I think, Lights will be coming on in the neighbors' houses. Somewhere down the block, already, a dog barks sharp and insistent, and a radio sings a sad song. I want it to be one that Elvis wrote but know it probably isn't.

Jeffrey has left the keys in the ignition. My hands start to itch and fidget at my sides, and I think how it would be the easiest thing in the world to slide into his seat, to head east—home—or straight north to the Reserve, that other home I've never seen. To just drive. But it would also be the hardest thing, and so I do slide over. I take the keys from the ignition, shut the pinging door, and join my husband in the yard.

It's too late, Jeffrey says. It's all too late now.

He has the sign half way out of its hole, and I stand there a moment, watching him shove, his hair in his eyes, his freckles stretching till they look like they might pop. He is pushing and pulling down low, working on the bottom of the post. I take the top of the post. I place my hands underneath the part that says *For Rent*. We have been married eight days. I move my hands closer to his, and I put my weight behind them, behind us, and we hang like that, quiet, the morning coming on.

Sight and Other Hazards

Mrs. Roubideaux from Apartment 212 knocked on the window, her fingers curved and yellowed like tusks, the hairs above her knuckles coarse and white and starting to curl. Her head was bent forward, and I swear, even through the glass, I heard her breath coming in snorts. Look at that, I thought, she's getting ready to charge. I leaned forward in my chair, my own fingers tensing into fists, and the second knock came—louder and sharper. Like I wasn't looking right at her. Like I missed it, somehow, the first time.

Ma jumped at the noise—the first time she'd moved that morning—then shrunk down into the white of her hospice bed. Her eyes, though, stayed blank, focused out somewhere past the window and Mrs. Roubideaux, past the row of cottonwoods that marked the edge of the grounds, past Holcomb, all of Holcomb County, maybe even all of West Texas, out into a place I was trying hard not to imagine.

For the past six months, we'd been having conversations about her dying, which went something like this:

Ma, you're going to be fine.

She sighed and looked around her hospice room as if just noticing it for the first time. Then she fixed her small, brown eyes on me—from the room to me and back—and let out a sigh of large and dramatic proportions, more than I would have thought her bone-thin body was capable of producing.

Just stick me up in a tree like in the old days, Ma said. The heat and the birds will take care of me.

It's quite an image, Ma wrapped tight in some blanket, hoisted up into the air, her gray, cotton-candy hair flying above her head like small, weird clouds that sunk too low. But as usual, she's more than a little off on her facts. It's true that some northern Indians did leave their dead in trees, and we're Blackfoot, Ramperts from Alberta originally, but we've been Southerners since Ma was just a girl. And I've looked in the library and online, and no where does it say any Indians from around here used to leave their almost-dead in trees. When I tried to reason with Ma, though, she just told her same stories.

Your Auntie Mavis went that way, Ma said. And my grandmother, too.

It's then that I pointed out we lived in West Texas now, where there were only cottonwoods with limbs too spindly to support even Ma's slight weight.

Ma, I said, there aren't any trees. You're just going to have to live.

Ma had stopped eating two weeks ago when the short, pregnant night nurse was fired. The short, pregnant night nurse had been building a college fund for her unborn child by sneaking whiskey into the hospital, serving it up one Dixie cup at a time. Between the cirrhosis and the cancer, Ma was dying anyway, the doctor said. He said it between glances at his watch. He said it wasn't a matter of choice, was instead a matter of time, but I knew better. This was my mother, who carried in and installed by herself every stove in every apartment of the complex she once managed, including the one Mrs. Roubideaux now used. If Ma wanted to live, she would.

I studied Ma's hunger-strike face for some change, but there was none. It stayed shrunken and hollow like a mouse who'd taken the poison, even when Mrs. Roubideaux knocked again, louder still, her fleshy face against the glass now, fogging it. Mrs. Roubideaux wore a clear, plastic rain bonnet, and the ends were knotted under her chin. It hadn't rained in fourteen days, and the bleached blue sky held nothing but the sun—big and round as a beach ball. When Mrs. Roubideaux knocked the fourth time, the plastic ends of her bonnet bobbed out from under her chins as if gasping for air and then went under.

The Roubideauxs were métis, the only other Indian family around here who came from where we did. This would seem like a natural bond but wasn't necessarily. Instead, when I was in school, the Roubideaux boys followed me around at recess, lifting up my skirt and commenting loudly on my underpants. Ma and Mrs. Roubideaux used to belong to the same card club, and every week, Ma would have a new story about Mrs. Roubideaux's stinginess, how she'd served only a small bag of potato chips, how she'd eaten the biggest ones herself. Still, we'd been to all the Roubideaux weddings, all the funerals, and when I graduated from high school, Mrs. Roubideaux made me a quilt so beautiful, so lively and bright that to this day, I have trouble believing it came from her hands.

I checked my cell phone and saw three missed calls, all from Mrs. Roubideaux, the first clocking in at 6:04 a.m. Someone better be dying, I thought, then looked sideways at Ma, guilty.

Mrs. Roubideaux lived on the other side of the building in the government apartments that Ma used to manage, that I now managed. The building used to be some big, grand hotel owned by the Holcombs, but it had been redone a few years back. The hotel was split in half, the east wing filled with rooms for those like my mother—the really dying. The west wing had apartments for the almost dead, the wish-they-were-dead, the old and disabled, and the very, very poor. All the tenants had to be poor by a state mandate, but their rent was scaled according to their income. They all knew roughly how much the other tenants paid, but Mrs. Roubideaux knew each person's amount, down to the dime.

When I replaced Ma as the caretaker last year, I handed out my number, telling everyone I would accept no calls before 8 a.m. or after 11 p.m. unless someone was dying. I handwrote Mrs. Roubideaux my phone number, slanting the last number so it looked more like a seven than a one. It was a nice, quiet week before she bullied Mr. Simpson in 219 into giving her the right number. The calls had been coming in twice a day since—Mr. Nelson in 215's rent being decreased by $11 a month; Mrs. Shuman (*that deaf woman*) in 212 burning her toast in a contraband oven; Mrs. Fielding in 208 having an overnight guest.

They're violating, Mrs. Roubideaux said. We've got regulations for a reason.

Her voice rose each time she said *reason*, high and squeaky at the start, shaking by the final *n*.

Ma, I said, I'm going to go find a tree for Mrs. Roubideaux.

Ma's hands were folded on top of the bed sheets—praying hands—and I wondered if the nurse had done that or if Ma had lifted them up herself. Usually, I pulled her hands out of the sheets for her each morning and rubbed them a little, starting with the palms and working my way down to the fingertips. For circulation, for good health.

It's going to be good, Ma, I said. You better get up and watch.

Ma moved her eyes and looked in the direction of me, at least, if not quite at me. Her praying hands shook a little, trying to draw me in, and her tongue snaked out between her lips.

I leaned in. What is it? I said.

She hadn't spoken since last week when she told the tall, sweaty nurse to please, for the love of God, start using deodorant. That was the last good day.

Ma, I said, is there something you need?

Her dry, cold hand brushed mine. Bud Light, she said. Gloria Jean, a Bud Light, please.

Her hands were on top of mine now, digging down, and I pulled mine out from under. No, Ma, I said. No liquor before noon. Not even beer.

Which had become a regulation for dying. But I wouldn't call it that out loud. Out loud, to the nurses and anyone else who asked, I said, She's fine. I said, We'll be going home one of these first days.

Outside, Mrs. Roubideaux still held vigil by Ma's window.

I snuck out the side door, closing it quietly behind me, and moved past the warming sidewalk, onto the drying up grass. I was sick of looking at it—everything dying—sick of summer and old people and heat. A vacation, up north, maybe, to visit some cousins. Somewhere with 70-degree temperatures, somewhere with rain.

I rounded the corner, and Mrs. Roubideaux knocked again, muttering something low under her breath. I clenched my fists, thinking how good it would feel to open then close them around her neck, but I was ashamed of the thought as quick as it came. It was not quite nine a.m., and I was homicidal. The sprinkler over by the cottonwoods spit and shrugged in fits. I watched its progress, thinking maybe I could make a run for it, make it all the way through the tree line before she turned.

But I waited too long, stuck there by the side of the building as if planted. Mrs. Roubideaux turned and began to make her way to me. I thought of how much dirt I could kick up if I fled, how she would choke on it, maybe, but I stood still. It was Mrs. Roubideaux who was stirring things up, anyway. With each step, she rotated her dull metal cane deep into the dry ground, leaving a series of small holes alongside the building in her wake.

Hot, isn't it? Mrs. Roubideaux said. I can't take much more, but they say it's going to rain.

If no one else was violating, the weather in West Texas always was. All conversations with her started with the weather, and many of the middles and ends focused there, too.

It's that blind man, again, Mrs. Roubideaux said. He's got this car out front of the building.

She leaned her weight onto the cane, and it wedged its way into a tuft of gray-green grass. She was out of breath. Sweat ran down her face, pooling briefly in the plastic under her chin before pouring out into the cleavage of her large, flowered dress. I looked away, unclenched my fists. Mr. Kessler, I thought. The blind man's name is Mr. Kessler.

I wondered how Ma was doing inside. I thought of her pushing herself up on her elbows and watching the scene, plotting ways to help me kill Mrs. Roubideaux or, even, picking out a new nurse to ask for beer, but I knew none of those things was happening.

That car, Mrs. Roubideaux said, is not up to code. It's up on blocks, and—

Mrs. Roubideaux, I said. I put my hands out in the universal *Please stop talking* gesture, but her mouth kept moving anyway.

—that's a clear violation, a hazard, even.

Over by the cottonwoods, the sprinkler sputtered to a stop, and Mrs. Roubideaux's voice boomed into the absence.

I'll bet that's a hazard. I'll bet Sheriff—

Mrs. Roubideaux, I said. I was nearly screaming now. My hands jabbed out in sharp, karate-like motions, then stopped short. I pulled them to my side where they fluttered like birds.

She was staring at me, at my hands. She shuffled back a little, dragging a trail into the dirt.

Mrs. Roubideaux, I said, even the blind man gets a parking spot.

She moved her mouth at me, but another sound rose up under it—a siren shrieking from the Sheriff's Department on Main Street, heading south, our way, wailing to a stop on the other side of the building. When I turned back to her, Mrs. Roubideaux was already halfway across the lawn, shuffle-running toward the apartments, a cloud of actual dust rising up behind her.

She beat me to the apartment side, somehow, despite being old and half-crippled. By the time I reached the double doors in front of the west wing, Mrs. Roubideaux was standing next to Sheriff McAdoo. She gestured toward the car, which was indeed up on blocks, then to me, then back toward the building. Its tall, brick form towered over the tiny lawn, the heat sending waves from the roof down to the straw-colored grass.

I wished for air conditioning, for the quiet of my car, parked only a few spaces from the blind man's. I could almost feel my fingers on the keys, the ignition turning, the air conditioner blasting. If somebody inside had fallen, I figured the ambulance would be here already. Most times, it took longer for the hearse, though, since the undertaker, Harv Jacobsen, had to close down and lock up his insurance shop. If he had a customer, it could take hours for the old muffler-less hearse to rumble down the street for a pick-up.

I wondered what Ma was doing back in her room. Maybe she was sweet-talking the new, tall nurse, trying to make up for past meanness, trying to score. It would be almost time for *The View*, and she liked to listen to the women argue, or at least I thought she did. I couldn't remember if I'd left the TV on for her, though, and I tried to visualize the screen—blank or filled—but failed.

Mrs. Roubideaux had hold of Sheriff's McAdoo's arm, was

trying to lead him to the car, but he kept turning away from her, kept turning back toward the middle of the building. The laundry room separated the building's east and west wings, was really more of a glorified hallway than a room. Somebody had propped open its door, and the dryer heat escaped in thick, cloud-like waves. Looking at them made my head hurt, made me long for a tall glass of cold water. Sheriff McAdoo shifted his considerable weight from one leg to the other, sweat beginning to stain his tan uniform shirt under the armpits and below the collar. I could hear Mrs. Roubideaux's high, nasal whine even over the air conditioner, but there was another sound underneath it.

Something like a moan came out of the heat and rose into a wail. I was past Mrs. Roubideaux and the sheriff, into the thick of it before I had time to think about what I might find. Inside the building, the heat from the dryer was worse than outdoors. The washer kicked and bucked in the center of the hall—somebody's sneakers or rug gone crazy—and thick steam poured out of the dryer, slickening the tile floor. I nearly slipped, had to reach for the door handle to steady myself.

In front of the washer stood the source of the noise. Mrs. Shuman leaned against it, rocking into it, her back to me, her wail now more like a hum. Across the hall from her stood Mr. Kessler, a basket of dirty laundry spilling out at his feet. Mrs. Shuman's wig flapped off the side of her head like a blackbird trying to take flight, and when I looked at Mr. Kessler again, I could see something in his hand, something black and stringy and not unlike hair.

I told you, Mrs. Roubideaux said. She materialized behind me, her plastic bonnet fogging on the inside, the sides of her dress now stuck to her sides. I told you that blind man was trouble.

Die, said the blind man. You old bitch, why don't you die.

Nobody said anything for a while after that, though Mrs. Roubideaux tensed, waiting for somebody to come to her defense, her big body hopeful and coiled.

Mr. Kessler, I said. Mr. Kessler—

But that was as far as I could get.

Mrs. Roubideaux sprang from the room, shoving past the sheriff and me, her cane slithering across wet tile. Sheriff McAdoo ran down what I'd missed, but I was already seeing it: how Mrs. Shuman was filling the machine when Mr. Kessler came in behind her with his clothes. How she had been unable to hear him coming up behind her. How he had been unable to see her there, bent over the machine. How his hands met her back instead of the machine, the tussle that ensued, the fake hair flying. How the whole scene was something I'd be seeing over and over, like a movie stuck on rewind. How I'd reconstruct it for Ma. How it might even make her smile.

Sheriff McAdoo tried not to smile as he told it. Mr. Simpson had called, he said. To report *shouting coming from the laundry.* Sheriff McAdoo covered his mouth with the back of his hand even though Mrs. Shuman wasn't looking, but Mr. Kessler heard it in his voice.

I don't see, Mr. Kessler said, I don't see what's so goddamned funny.

Which set us off even more. We leaned into the dryer, which had quit its thumping, and wiped tears from the corners of our eyes.

Christ, the sheriff said. I thought I'd seen everything.

Outside, Mrs. Roubideaux was waiting. It's too hot, she said. It's too hot, and I want to know if that deaf woman's filing.

The sheriff stared hard at the tops of his dull, brown shoes.

He should be arrested, she said.

I stared at Mrs. Roubideaux. No, I said. Mrs. Roubideaux, nobody's filing anything.

I grinned at the sheriff, at her. The sun beat down. I had forgotten my sunglasses, and I thought if I looked straight up, my eyes might scorch. Then I could live in the apartments instead of taking care of them.

Mrs. Shuman staggered by us on the way to her apartment, her wig now straightened, her moans stuffed down deep so there was silence, at least for a little while. But then I heard it—the muffler-less rumbling as Harv Jacobsen rounded the corner, heading past us back to the funeral home, coming from the other side of the wing.

The nurse with the sweat stains met me at the door to Ma's room.

I'm sorry, she said. She leaned forward in that consoling way like I'm sure she'd done so many times, and her chubby hands folded against her belly and unfolded like they couldn't find a place to rest.

We're all so sorry, she said, and it came out like she meant it, like she really was sorry. I marveled at that for a moment, at how she leaned into me but did not touch me, at how her hands seemed to be disembodied, out of sync.

I'd set this up with the nurses beforehand—how if Ma went

and they couldn't reach me they should call Harv. I hadn't thought it could happen like this—so fast while I wasn't looking—and I hadn't thought it would matter, anyway, seeing her in her bed or at Harv's place, but of course now it did.

The nurse moved on down the hallway under the glare and hum of fluorescence. I passed through the doorway and sat on the edge of the bed, which had been stripped. A full plastic cup of water sat on the bedside table, its crooked straw bending out toward me. It hurt to look at it. I should have done it, I thought. Should have, just once, brought what she'd asked for.

The TV flickered from its place up in the corner, and I was glad I had remembered to turn it on. At least she had that. I was sitting there on the bare mattress, working over its curves when I felt it give a little behind me.

It was Mrs. Roubideaux, sitting behind me, her cane in one hand, the other at her bonnet, pulling on its ends. She had a look on her face that I couldn't place.

Your mother, she said. Your mother always could talk about the weather.

And then her mouth went quiet.

Outside the window, the sprinkler kicked back on, and I could see someone had moved it closer to the cottonwoods, to where it should have been all along. The roots were getting wet, though not very, since the day was closing in on noon, and the heat soaked up the moisture almost before it left the sprinkler. I could imagine the sound of it—spitting out water in fits and starts—and I leaned forward as if to catch it but could not.

Mrs. Roubideaux dragged her cane along the tile floor,

making a figure-eight-style pattern, showing a thin layer of dust when I would have sworn the floor was clean. She made a guppy sound behind me like she'd opened her mouth then closed it fast, and that—the silence—was what I'd seen in her eyes, too. The sun beat down on the sprinkler, moving the water independent of us, but we were part of it somehow, too. We were quiet there on the bed, our hands folded into our separate laps, our fingers flexing and grasping, overlapping and settling like waves.

Flight

Clarissa lay on her back, the box spring's cold metal inches from her nose, the rough weave of the St. David's Hotel carpet itching the backs of her knees. She clutched the roll of duct tape up to her chest, pressed her fingers around the loose, sticky corner and released. There was a small, sucking noise, like a baby letting go of its bottle. The man's grey pant legs and worn brown shoes slowed next to the bed, next to where Clarissa lay. Her fingers stuck around the duct tape and stayed, this time.

The man's legs turned in a circle, once, twice, three times around like a dog trying to settle down for the night. Over in the corner, the heater rumbled on, and Clarissa felt its warmth against her legs. She hadn't realized how cold it was until she felt the warmth. I should have put on pants, she thought, but it was early October, that time when the weather could do anything, and it had been warm when she'd left the house. Clarissa felt the carpet, the stick of the tape, and she slowed her breathing further. Quiet. Quiet now.

She thought of playing hide and seek with her little brother Derby. How she'd fold herself into the clothes hamper though it was getting to be a tight fit. How he'd look all through the house, toddling like a penguin through each room until she'd clear her throat or cough. Then he'd make his way to the bathroom. Clarissa could hear him pulling back the shower curtain, shaking its plastic between his soft, round fists. She'd cough again and he'd turn, pulling up the hamper lid, and she'd unfold, lifting him up with her, his flat, round face creased with a smile, mirroring her own.

But that was before. She tried not to see Derby the way he'd been that last time—the vacant stare as he pushed himself back from the kitchen table and started the three feet to the refrigerator. How he'd stalled out one-foot shy. How he'd limped in circles, his left leg dragging, a lame horse drawn in miniature.

Clarissa closed her eyes against it, and when she opened them, Derby was gone, and the man's legs were bending at the knees. She could see them through the edge of the stiff, polyester bedspread, which flapped like a curtain as he knelt. And then the curtain was rising.

Clarissa checked the mailbox for the second time that afternoon. The July sun beat down, wilting the oaks and maples that lined the Rapid City neighborhood, the sun burning pale tourists on their way to Mount Rushmore, searing all of western South Dakota, including the dull grey metal of the mailbox handle. But Clarissa had come prepared. She'd taken one of her aunt Vickie's potholders and now wrapped it around the handle, looking both ways to be sure no one was watching. Clarissa had been to the mailbox twice a day since she'd come to live with Uncle Leroy and his wife Vickie. That's forty times, she thought, thirty-nine with no letter from the southeastern part of the state, the small town just off the Lakota reservation where her mother and brother still lived. This time she'd take the mail into the house before she looked at it—break the pattern, start some new luck.

Clarissa tucked the potholder into the waistband of her shorts and pulled her shirt over it. She looked both ways, but it was too hot for anyone to be out, and the nearby lawns were quiet, only the air conditioners buzzing and humming. Theirs was the smallest house on the block, but Leroy kept the grass the same length as the other, bigger yards.

I don't want them talking about us, Vickie said. I don't want to hear a word about those Indians bringing the property values down.

Clarissa pushed through the front door, into the cool of the living room, past Vickie who sat in her recliner in front of the TV. She had just finished a twelve-hour shift at the hospital and hadn't yet changed out of her grey-green nurses' scrubs. The potholder was warm against Clarissa's belly, and she passed through the dining room fast, leaving the mail on the table. In the kitchen, she opened the drawer next to the stove quietly, placing the potholder in with the others, straightening the stack before pushing in the drawer.

She could hear Vickie in the next room, clicking channels without pause, and Clarissa breathed a little slower. She backed into the dining room, turning to the stack of mail lying facedown on the table, and her breath again started to come in short gasps. She leaned her slim hips against the table, her hazel eyes registering hope. Clarissa could feel Vickie watching her through the open doorway though Vickie pretended to watch the screen, pretended to be comfortable sitting there with their big Newfoundland Sue at her feet, wagging and slobbering until Vickie reached a chubby hand down to scratch behind his right ear, sending him into tail-thumping overdrive.

Clarissa smiled at Sue who thumped his tail faster. Uncle Leroy had won Sue in a poker game over at the hotel where he worked. He liked to sing to the dog, his boy named Sue, liked to tell Vickie that Sue was the only boy they'd ever have if they didn't get started here pretty soon.

Clarissa touched the envelopes. They were still warm. She turned them over, started to flip through the small stack.

Your mother's not going to write, Vickie said. Don't kid yourself.

Clarissa was on the last envelope, a bright yellow one marked PAST DUE.

I know that, she said.

She turned her back to Vickie and the television, her hand resting on a white envelope, fingering its edge. It held the VISA logo and was addressed to Victoria Roubideaux or Current Resident.

Uncle Leroy swung into the kitchen through the back door, his cell phone at his ear. He paced and hissed into the phone.

You already get plenty. You already get a goddamn 'nough, do you hear me?

He punched a button hard and threw the phone down onto the counter next to the coffeepot, which bounced on impact.

Everyone always has their hand out, Leroy said.

He watched the coffeepot jiggle, not turning until it settled, and it was then that he saw Clarissa leaning into the table, her eyes fixed on the linoleum at his feet. He stepped back, startled, his face letting her know he hadn't meant for her to overhear, letting her know she was another worry, another hand. Leroy lowered his eyes, kicked the bottom of the refrigerator, and sucked his breath in fast before stumbling out the back door.

Clarissa stared at the scuffmark his boot made, folded the envelope lengthwise, and slipped it up her sleeve.

The heat stayed through August, through the beginning of Clarissa's freshman year of high school, wilting everything and everyone, plastering Clarissa's long brown hair to the back of her neck. It was the first Friday of the semester, second period algebra class, and the weekend dangled before her, just out of reach above the substitute's head in cartoon bubble words like *help* and *me*. The woman's bobbed, dishwater hair bounced along with her chin as she read the roll. Clarissa wondered if Vickie was home yet from her night shift at the hospital, if she was sitting in her recliner, feet propped up on Sue. Clarissa wondered if the mail had come yet, and embarrassment, not unlike longing, crept up her collar to her cheeks.

She was staring into the space above the substitute's head, and the room had gone quiet.

Clarissa? said the sub. Clarissa Roubi, Roubi—

Clarissa came to and gave the sub a flat-handed, beauty queen wave that drew a laugh from someone behind her. The sub, apparently, saw only the name.

Clarissa. Like the novel, the sub said. The world's longest novel. The blank stare Clarissa offered up seemed only to fuel the velocity of the chin nodding and hair bobbing. The woman clearly wanted to talk about books or at least not to talk about algebra since they were twenty-two minutes into the class and still on paper shuffling and roll taking.

Yes? *Clarissa.* You know, surely. The woman gave a deep, head-shaking sigh. It's a *million* words.

Clarissa shrugged, looking around the room for help, but all the other students were suddenly fascinated by their desktops, fingertips, and sneakers.

I'll bet you're named for the heroine, right?

Clarissa shrugged again, but she could feel the embarrassment starting up again, creeping up the back of her shirt. Someone behind her snickered. It occurred to her with ever-widening horror that the woman was now trying to draw her out. As if in response, the sub smiled brightly.

A grandmother, then? It's such an unusual name for a young girl.

More snickers from behind and one half-smothered guffaw. Clarissa, this time, didn't even offer a shrug but instead examined the tops of her canvas shoes, which she noticed were beginning to fray at the edges.

Well, said the sub. I guess we'll move on, then. Ahem. Boyd Sampson?

It was too late, though.

The junkie whore, Clarissa said.

Excuse me? replied the sub.

All eyes now rose from tennis shoes and fingertips to focus on Clarissa.

The junkie whore from the house next door, Clarissa said. The one my mom thought my dad was screwing. Before he left.

It didn't matter that it wasn't true—that she was pretty sure she was named for one of her dad's aunts, that there had been no junkies or whores anywhere near the small house she and her family had lived in, back when they were a family. The story did what it was supposed to. The chin bobbing stopped; all sound, all motion stopped. The sweat from Clarissa's hairline started to pool and run, but she couldn't stop herself.

That's who I'm named for.

She was already out of her seat, heading toward the door, fingering the smooth plastic of the card wedged into her jeans' front pocket as she spoke the last words. The door swung closed behind her, and the hallway held only the gunmetal lockers and waxed linoleum squares. So she addressed them. You know, she said. It's funny.

The days began to cool after that, and in the mornings, the lawns stiffened with the weight of the first few frosts. Every weekday morning for the next four weeks, Clarissa took the C bus to the stop before the school, and there she switched to the B line. The B line took her past young mothers swinging and strolling with their children in College and Horace Mann Parks, out to the city limits and the Rushmore Mall where there were shoes. Store after store, row after row of neat cardboard boxes filled with shoes—and she bought what she saw, what she liked, but mostly, she bought what she thought Derby might see or like if he were able. If he could still hold his head upright. Then, at 2:45 p.m. each day, she hopped the B line back to the stop near the school where she met bus C to take her home—just as the rest of the school kids lined their parents' doorways.

She'd been absent for not quite two weeks when a woman had called from the school. Vickie was out grocery shopping, but Clarissa turned the machine's volume down anyway and put her ear to its speaker before playing and replaying the message. She dialed the number the secretary had left for the principal, hoping he was answering his own phone. In the message, the secretary sounded like Vickie with her crisp, clipped speech, always hurrying toward the ends of words as if she couldn't cut them off fast enough. She might be hard to fool. Clarissa had seen the principal's office, complete with the PrinciPAL is your PAL placard. She hoped he would be in.

Mrs. Roubideaux, said the principal, what can I do for you?

It was easy after that, effortless. Mrs. Roubideaux explained how it just hadn't worked out with that Clarissa, how she had been more trouble than anyone possibly could have anticipated, how it was too bad—terrible, really—but they'd been forced to send her back where she came from, and so could he please forward her file at his first convenience? Clarissa hauled out the grownup-sounding clichés, being careful to speak as if she were late for something, as if she wanted to kill the-*ly* at the end of *possibly*, the *one* at the end of *anyone*.

The first Friday afternoon in September, Clarissa opened the front door of Vickie and Leroy's house quietly, her backpack full of shoes weighing down her left shoulder, throwing her off-balance. So she wasn't ready for Vickie who should have been in the back bedroom sleeping off the night shift but, instead, filled the doorway, her dark eyes popping. Vickie grabbed Clarissa's backpack, pulling her and it through the doorway and into the living room, sending Clarissa to the thin, tan carpet. Clarissa's suitcases lay open beside the coffee table. Small shoes spilled out and covered the carpet like freckles on skin. Sue licked Clarissa's face and pawed at her to pet him.

You, Vickie said.

Her voice was soft, low, like she couldn't get her bearings. She waved the VISA bill in the air near her face absently, as if fanning herself, looking from the shoes to the bill's last line: $1433.62. Vickie shook her head and gaped at Clarissa, who crouched next to the coffee table among the shoes.

Trouble, Vickie said, I—

Clarissa looked over at Sue who was whining and trying without success to wedge himself under the couch. She had expected yelling, screaming, maybe even a slap. This pale, speechless Vickie was frightening. So something like relief worked its way into Clarissa's limbs when Vickie grabbed her arm, pulled her from the floor, and led her to the back bedroom's walk-in closet, shoving her in, closing the double doors behind her and securing them with a chair tucked under the handles.

There, Vickie said, finding her voice. You like shoes so much—there you go.

The bottom of the closet was full already—suitcases, an old sewing machine, a basketball—but shoes took up the most space, Leroy's size twelve work boots and tennis shoes, Vickie's hardly used, pointy toed pumps and no longer white nurse's shoes. Clarissa shoved them aside, piling as many as she could into the corners. She squatted beneath the arms of faded flannels, the starched legs of nursing scrubs worn thin. She pushed on the middle of the double doors at the place where they met, where they should buckle, but the chair held them. She could hear Sue's slurpy breathing on the other side of the doors, could feel his tail thump against the carpet. Clarissa slipped a hand under the door and scratched a hind leg. Sue thumped frantically.

You, Vickie said. Get away from there.

Clarissa felt the floor give as Sue hefted himself up, and she heard the click-clack of his nails across the kitchen's linoleum and then the smack of plastic meeting back door as his giant doggie door slammed shut behind him. Vickie turned the TV on in the living room and was flipping channels as if she might not get another chance, the sounds bouncing and booming and bouncing again.

It was dark in the closet, and Clarissa's eyes were closing though she tried to will them open. Shopping always made her tired, what she imagined real illness felt like—draggy limbs, greasy hair, pale skin, bad breath. Something about mall air and light wore on her, and, soon, she slept, curled against the sewing machine.

Hours later, Clarissa jumped awake in the dark of the

closet, the house now quiet. It was hard to tell how much time had passed exactly, but she thought it must be night by now, that Vickie must have gone to work.

Vickie? she said. Her voice sounded strange and thin, even to her, like it might be coming out of somebody else. Anybody home?

When no answer came, Clarissa grabbed a stray hanger and wiggled down to the closet floor, pushing on the sewing machine until it moved over just enough so she could lie on her side, facing the doors. She sweated a little from nerves and effort as she swung the hanger out, trying to hook a chair leg. On the third try, it caught hold, and the chair toppled sideways to the floor with a satisfying thud. Without the chair to hold them together, the thin, cheap doors popped open under the stress of one good kick, and Clarissa spilled out into Vickie and Leroy's bedroom, into more quiet and dark.

The bedside clock read 2:53, and with Vickie safely in the middle of her shift, Clarissa sank onto the carpet in front of the closet, her heartbeat slowing. She grabbed the old flannel shirt from the closet floor and wiped the sweat from her face. The shirt was soft like the pajamas Derby had worn that last night. Clarissa had felt the thin fabric rub into her skin when she dragged Derby from the house into their mother's car and then again when she dragged him out, into the blinking lights and sterile white of Indian Health Services.

By the time her mother arrived from her job cleaning houses twenty miles away, the initial tests were back, revealing some sort of poisoning, a chemical not unlike formaldehyde. Celia's eyes first had gone blank, then accusatory, then apologetic three days later when Derby's best friend Bobby Frausto was rushed in with bleeding gums and slurred speech. And the next day, it had been Krista Fulton, head lolled to the right as if knocked loose by a sharp left hook—on and on, until two-thirds of Derby's Head Start class had visited the hospital.

It was three more long weeks of tests, of walking the smooth, sterile linoleum corridors, before the source was traced: a mislabeled jug of cleaning solution used to sanitize toothbrush handles at the Head Start, the poison traveling through the plastic into the bristles, into the preschoolers' mouths as they brushed and rinsed away their afternoon snacks.

The problems varied. Not all spun in left-leaning circles like Derby. Not all had neurological damage. But that's how Clarissa imagined them: sixteen four-year olds spinning left in concentric circles, wearing down the outside edges of their left shoes until only holes were left, until their feet were wide open, susceptible to every imaginable kind of breeze.

Clarissa approached the alley behind the St. David's Hotel and Leroy's basement bar with four dollars and thirty-seven cents in her left jeans' pocket, a butter knife up her right sleeve. She had fingered the serrated edge as she shuffle-ran the four blocks from the house, her stick legs stiff and numb from captivity. The St. David's Hotel, a tall, brick square, took up most of the block and shared its back alley and garbage bins with the Chamber of Commerce building, a two-story, smaller scale version of the hotel.

Even the back alley of this place strove for intimidation.

Its grey-green garbage containers had been lined up flush with the soft yellow brick, the bright blue recycling bins stacked perfectly like LEGOS. But an old orange-striped tomcat lay on top of the stack, hissing, and the place smelled like an alley—old cigarettes, sour milk, spilled beer.

Clarissa had been to the upstairs levels with their chandeliers and butter-oak paneling many times but never to the basement below. She'd followed Leroy once, intending to slip in behind him somehow, but after watching him jimmy the back door's lock with a screwdriver, she had been depressed and headed on home. He'd been managing the housekeeping crew upstairs for twelve years, had been running things downstairs for the last four, and still, he needed a screwdriver because management changed the locks frequently, and he was not quite management.

Clarissa pulled the butter knife from her sleeve and crept toward the door. It swung open as she reached it and two large, white men stumbled out, drunk. She stepped in under the biggest one's hairy arm and hurried down the creaking stairs, the bad smells increasing with each step.

The stairs opened out onto a square, low-ceilinged room, no more than fifteen-feet wide or long. It was smaller than she'd thought it would be, given the size of the hotel, and less like a bar than the basement of some old man's house. Pieces of plywood lay two thick on cinder blocks along one wall with a few occupied bar stools in front of them. Men much like the ones Clarissa passed on the stairs—middle aged, white or mixed blood, eyes drawn down—overflowed folding chairs. They slumped beefy forearms onto card tables, nursing whiskey or slamming beers. Sue lay under the card table closest to the door, his paws across a large, pale man's feet. The dog thumped his tail when Clarissa passed, and the man scratched the dog behind his ear.

Leroy stood behind the bar, pouring whiskey into a shot glass. Clarissa approached.

That for me? she said. She put her hands on her hips and walked the last few feet to the bar, trying for a swagger but missing.

Leroy shook his head and handed the shot to the man on the last bar stool. Clarissa pulled up a stool and waited while a young man, dressed for upstairs in a white shirt, dark pants, and a green-and-gold vest, handed Leroy a key card.

Room 214. That Holcomb guy from Texas. Checked out, paid for, but his stuff's still there. You want the girls to clean it or what?

Leroy shrugged. It's slow. We'll give him a couple days.

Green vest nodded and gave Clarissa an appraising look that she returned with a scowl. She turned to Leroy.

She's been keeping me in the closet, you know.

He polished a pint glass. Clarissa squared her shoulders and tried for a self-righteous tone, though, in truth, she knew she was as much to blame as Vickie.

Your bitch of a wife has been keeping me locked in a closet while you're down here playing bartender.

She shook her right leg, partly for emphasis, partly to shake out the tingle. Her voice was shrill, heading for ear splitting. Two men at Sue's card table turned to stare. Leroy raised an eyebrow but kept polishing.

In the goddamn closet, Leroy.

She was shouting, now, her voice gone stranger still. It was the only sound other than the scrape of metal chair legs on cement floor as the men began to realize there was a show.

Leroy smiled but his face was tight, the lines around his eyes deeper than she remembered them being even the day before. My niece, he said. He swung his bar towel in a wide gesture, and the door swung open with it as if synchronized.

Ladies and gentlemen, my niece, fresh out of the—

The commotion drowned his feeble joke. The orange-striped tomcat stood in the doorway, rubbing against the legs of a tall man, and Sue rose up under the card table with all his 110 pounds, arching his back and bouncing the table onto its side before woofing and giving chase.

The place erupted with cries of *Sue!* and *Alright!* Clarissa would have bet those men had never moved faster than a shuffle, but there they were, leaping up collectively, scattering folding chairs and giving chase.

The men followed the dog, who followed the cat, and Clarissa found herself alone in the bar except for one old white man who snored and shook at a back table. The key card lay on the plywood next to the towel and gleaming glasses. It was nearing 5 a.m., and when she closed her eyes, the decision seemed easy enough.

Room 214 contained a clean, queen-sized bed, the same butter-oak woodwork and dense, dark green carpet as the lobby, with walls papered in green and gold flowers. A suitcase was perched on the dresser, but it was locked tight. Over the suitcase hung the room's centerpiece—an enormous and cheap reproduction of a painting entitled The Spirit of the Dakotas. It was a medley of sorts, with downtown Sioux

Falls in the upper right corner, its falls below, the ridiculous
Mitchell Corn Palace dead center.

It was the left side that drew Clarissa in, though. In the
upper corner across from the center ran Mount Rushmore,
and below it in the lower left corner, Indians on horseback
chased each other in circles in the space that now was the
monument's parking lot.

Clarissa had it down, out of the glass, and spread out on
the bed before really deciding what to do next. She opened
all the dresser's drawers, searching but coming up empty.
In the bedside drawer, a roll of duct tape and sharp scissors
bookended the Bible. She paused before picking them up,
not wanting to think about why Mr. Room 214 might have
put them there.

She severed west from east with one long cut, and then she
lay down on the bed, holding the west above her, studying it.
The east and the reservation with her hometown just outside
it were included, lay facedown on the dark green shag, but
Clarissa didn't want to think about them either. Instead, she
rolled onto her stomach with the picture before her, going
to work with the scissors.

The sun had started to rise by the time she finished; it
bled fuchsia, orange, and red onto the frost-covered grass
outside, through the tightly drawn blinds. Clarissa felt the
warmth play across her face, and her eyes started to close
though she knew it was cold outside, that the cold would be
staying now, that there was no going back. She closed her
eyes against it, and she drifted into the street noise coming
up from below—the honks and thuds and bleats of the day's
beginning.

She imagined her mother's car was part of the noise, the last slam her car door. Celia burst into the basement bar and shook Leroy by the collar till he pointed up the stairs, muttered 214. This was fantasy, of course, and even in the last moments before sleep, Clarissa knew the difference. Leroy didn't, for example, own a shirt with a collar, but still, Clarissa could see her mother's long, thin legs, her brother's short, chubby ones taking the stairs fast, side by side—his working double time to keep up. Their progress was steady, and they climbed up and up in a straight line, but the top landing seemed to move, up and up, higher and higher, always just out of reach.

Clarissa was almost asleep when she heard the footsteps thunking double-time down the hall then stopping fast outside her door. She jumped down from the bed and scooted under it, the duct tape in her left hand, a young Lakota on a pony in her right.

The rest of the painting lay scattered around the room—Indians on horseback riding atop the TV, on the cover of the air conditioner, on the Bible, which lay in the bedside drawer Clarissa had left open. It had felt good, leaving it open, but it had felt scary too—no one to tell her to shut it, no one to mind things were so far out of place. It had felt good, cutting the painting apart though she knew she was too old to make paper dolls, too old for such games, which weren't that much fun without Derby, anyway.

Clarissa could hear the man moving around the room, could hear him fingering the dolls. He was whistling low under his breath, and she thought it could be a happy sound, but she knew it was not. And then his legs were bending, and she was holding her breath, counting in her head to see how long she could hold it all in. She was telling herself these were her mother's legs, that she had just forgotten what they looked like. That it had been too long. She was telling herself she was going home. And then the bedspread's curtain was rising, and Clarissa was rising, too. She was on her way home now—she was going home.

Looking for Boll Weevil

At six in the morning, forty miles south of the Twin Cities, I jerked awake in the cold and dark of the bus our school group was sharing with a bunch of touring senior citizens. I was a long way from home, and the air felt different than West Texas air. It was thicker, more humid, and it smelled different, too, like pine trees, maybe, even through the mix of teenager and old people smells circulating around the bus. My niece slept beside me, her face scrunched into a sleepy frown, thin hands clutching the blanket up under her chin.

Two days ago, my sister Diane had called from St. Paul. It was four in the afternoon, a bright April day, the unseasonable sun blanching the cotton fields, searing the manzanitas in the canyon. My niece Sandra's fifth grade class was heading out on a bus for the Rosebud Reservation in South Dakota. My sister, a trip sponsor, had been promoted at her job. She was now too important to ride a bus to South Dakota. I was unemployed, and I never had been that important. Still, it was cold in South Dakota sometimes in April. Still, I didn't necessarily want to do Diane any favors.

We are métis, Roubideaux, from near the Blood Reserve in Alberta, and Sandra's father Pete is Blackfoot. I didn't see why Sandra had to get on a bus and go all the way to South Dakota to see some Indians.

Look, Diane said, they've been sponsoring Grandma Claw since first grade.

I didn't know we had a grandmother named Claw, I said. Neat.

It's a school trip, Diane said, graduation into middle school, a rite of passage.

I sighed into the phone.

I'll buy your plane ticket here, Diane said.

I sighed again, louder this time, but Diane already was talking over me, explaining the rest fast—how the children were part of this Sponsor an Elder program, how they gave *Grandma Claw* food and yarn to make blankets or rugs or something, how then they went on a big celebration trip and met *their* elder. I opened my mouth to continue the arguing, but Diane was holding out the phone, and I could hear Sandra crying. Before long, I had my instructions: how I was to bring sleeping bags and pillows, pack sandwiches and fresh fruit but no cigarettes, no booze. Diane said that last part twice, hands clicking double-time against the receiver.

The bus lurched and shrugged down the highway, and a silver-haired woman stumbled in the aisle up front. With her wild hair and hunched shoulders, she looked a little like Bobby

Jo, my landlady back in West Texas. In exchange for cheap rent and a house on 500 acres at the top of Blanco Canyon, I watered cottonwood and fruit-bearing trees, peach and apple, and pear, mostly pear, row on row of pear, stretching out under the hot West Texas sun.

What are you going to do with all those pears? I had asked Bobby Jo the first time I visited the place.

We, she said. What are *we* going to do with all those pears.

It was unnatural, all those trees out there on the high plains, all the watering. It was almost as bad as Indians riding a bus 400 miles to gawk at other Indians. But I had seen the way Bobby Jo looked at the trees. Every Sunday she drove out from Lubbock and moved her aging body tree to tree, row to row, checking the water hoses and sprinklers, her hands open, her voice rising in what could be construed as prayer.

It was the boll weevils she found unnatural, and, technically, she was right. The cotton-destroying snout beetle was native only to Mexico and Central America and wasn't introduced into West Texas until 1892, shortly after the Comanche were introduced to small pox, cholera, and General Mackenzie.

They've done so much damage in such a short time, Bobby Jo said.

Yes, I said. They have.

But it was only April, and the boll weevils were still in diapause, I hoped, were sleeping the spring away, waiting for the lasting heat of July. In the spring, I watered the trees and checked the boll weevil traps for freak, unseasonable activity, which the kind of heat we'd been having could inspire.

I worried over the possibilities, and the Bobby Jo look-alike continued to wander, up and down the aisle, one shoe untied. I wondered if the pear trees had gone dry, if the boll weevils were waking up and flying, taking over the cotton in my absence. The woman paused by our row, shoe now tied.

My shoe, she slurred, my shoe.

It's tied now, I said. See?

My shoe, she said. Her face contorted, her voice rising. My shoe!

Okay, I said. All right.

I reached down and untied the shoe closest to me. It was standard old lady issue, tan and thick soled. I leaned in close to retie it and smelled new leather, but the laces were already worn smooth and thin.

There, I said. I leaned back in my seat, the lace double-knotted.

The woman shuffled away, down the aisle toward the back of the bus. My shoe, she said, my shoe.

I wished Diane were here. I'd ask her if we could give this woman a blanket and all go home. If it would make every-one feel better, we could even call this woman *Grandma*. I thought about asking Nancy, the trip leader, but she was quiet, sitting up front by herself behind the driver, and besides, I hadn't figured out why she was here yet, if she was in it for the children, wanted to see an Indian, wanted to be an Indian, or what. She was dark-skinned and dark-eyed, but her hair was blond—the opposite of me with my pale skin and dark hair. Together, I thought, we could make somebody's idea of a complete Indian.

Sandra stirred beside me.

Are we there yet?

She brushed her dark hair away from her face with the back

of her hand, eyes squinting in the strange not quite dark that was bus light.

No, I said. But only a couple hours to go.

Promise? She had her mother's eyes—dark and doubtful and angled up slightly at the corners, even in sleep.

Promise, I said, and she turned back to the window, burrowing down under the blanket.

It was late afternoon by the time we got to Mission and the reservation after letting off the seniors at the Corn Palace in Mitchell. The plan was to eat sandwiches at the casino outside of town, meet our elder, and attend some sort of fifth grade graduation ceremony the teachers had concocted. I was curious about having snacks with fifth graders at a casino, but when I said as much, four of the five other women in the group scowled, shot me a look that said, *You're not a mother, are you?*

They're giving us a deal, Nancy said. It's the off-season.

As we pulled into the parking lot, though, I was having a hard time imagining this place was ever *in* season. The concrete lot rose up from the highest point on the rolling plains, majestic, I guessed, but nearly empty. The lot could easily hold a section of cotton but now held only a handful of cars, huddled together. Rows of baby pine lined the shiny, new building, making something like a windrow except they were only about knee high. They listed out from their shallow, half-filled holes.

The bus shuddered to a stop just as a small tree near the front of the line broke loose and skidded across the concrete, flying end on end, out over the nearest low-lying ridge, and was gone.

Sandra perched on a seat up front, shoulders hunched forward. I could feel her frown before she turned around and gave it to me. I shrugged. This wasn't my idea. The wind rattled the bus windows, a million teeth chattering in unison, and Sandra's frown turned to a scowl. The corners of my face lifted in a feeble attempt at a smile, and we sat there a while, her scowling, me mock smiling, the rest of the children and parents gathering their things. They were all making happy noises like they hadn't noticed the wind.

I could rent a car, I thought, and be back with the cotton-woods and boll weevils by bedtime if I drove straight through. Tomorrow morning I could be sitting out by the canyon in the sunshine, melting the plastic smile right off my face.

You coming?

It was Nancy, standing over me, my bag in her left hand, another larger one slung over her right shoulder. You know, she said, you can smoke in the casino part of the casino.

She looked over her shoulder before shaking a pack of Virginia Slim Menthols at me, but we were the only ones left on the bus. Outside, Sandra skipped along with a friend, their hair swirling above their heads in the fierce wind. They broke into a run when they reached the pine trees and soon were swallowed up by the building. I took a cigarette from Nancy's pack and followed her down the steps, out into the cold.

We stood in the casino entryway, assaulted with its sounds and smells—the clicks and whirs of the slots, the stale mix of cigarettes and old people armpits.

Ugh, I said, lighting up my cigarette, this is awful.

Nancy turned back to me, grinning, hers already lit.

Arrows overhead pointed the ways to the restaurant,

hotel, casino, and swimming pool. Look, I said, the four directions.

Nancy pulled a roll of quarters from her jacket, and we chose north for casino. The others must have already gone south to the restaurant because we were the only ones from our group in sight. The place was empty except for the white-shirted, black-pants and-tie-wearing waitresses and dealers, and the old people—they huddled in front of the slots and tables, the women both Indian and white in polyester, the men in seed corn or cowboy hats and thin, plaid shirts.

I studied the carpet's geometric design, how the pattern led in all directions but also seemed to circle back to the spot where I stood. I leaned my back against a slot machine, my head in my hands, dizzy, not quite able to catch my breath.

You're not going to win like that, Nancy said.

She was still grinning, shaking her half-empty roll of quarters, and there was another roll in her other hand. A woman with dark, permed hair and a round tray brought Nancy a Coke. She handed me one of her rolls and pulled a flask from her pocket. I tried to look away, tried to focus somewhere else, but before long I turned back, swallowed hard and nodded at her, at the flask.

Forty minutes passed like that—drinks and cigarettes and the whir of the machines—and then the door opened and a tall, dark-haired man blew through it, brushing snow from his collar, shaking it off his cowboy hat.

We moved from the machines to the window, rubbed the fog from it. Snow blew down crazily, covering the baby trees, the huddled cars, the bus.

Crap, Nancy said.

Seriously, I said, it's ninety degrees at home.

Nancy laughed, throwing back her head, her dirty blond hair falling everywhere. You're stuck here, she said, laughing harder, and you're not even the mom.

I gulped down the last of my drink, and Nancy did the same.

Come on, she said.

The kids and other parents or parent substitutes sat at booths and rectangular tables, finishing off their sandwiches. I scanned the room but didn't see Sandra. I looked over at Nancy to ask if she saw her, but Nancy's face had gone slack.

Rochelle? she yelled. Has anyone seen Rochelle?

The faces turned, and my face, already flushed from the drinks, grew brighter still. The oldest woman in the group stood and shuffled over to us. Somebody's grandmother, I thought, as she took Nancy and me each by an arm and hustled us into the corner where people had hung their coats. I was trying to remember if I'd brought a coat or just a jacket when the old woman said it—*We thought they were with you*—when it hit me that Rochelle must be Sandra's friend, that they were both, somehow, gone.

The mothers became a flurry of limbs and bobbed hair, pushing their kids into the opposite end of the restaurant. Like we're contagious, I thought, but then it occurred to me that we *had* been drinking. That we'd lost our kids.

I wished I could will myself home—the lawn chair, the sunshine, even the boll weevils calling me back. I wished Diane were here and then was glad she wasn't. She was going to kill me, I thought, and then felt guilty for thinking only of that and the throbbing that was starting up on both sides of my head.

The old woman jabbered away to the kids—*Did any of you notice*—then shuffled back to our corner to report the non-information. No one had seen anything. Nancy leaned onto her knees, her face two shades paler. I'd lost the sunshine now, was thinking of snow banks, exposed limbs, frozen fingers. I tried to push the thought away, to focus this time, to try harder.

Look, I said, they have to be somewhere.

It's snowing, Nancy said. It's snowing and—

I circled around the old woman to Nancy's side. I took her hand.

Come on, I said, we'll find them.

The old woman stayed in the south with the children, who sat at her feet on the restaurant floor, and the rest of us fanned out in the other directions. This time, Nancy and I headed west to the swimming pool. This time, I led.

I hurried through the glass door, down the narrow hallway, smelling the chlorine already. My heart beat fast under my shirt and I was starting to sweat, but I didn't tell Nancy. She was scared, mumbling something about a custody fight and being a terrible mother, about never having taken Rochelle to a powwow.

The blue-green pattern on the carpet zigged and zagged, the geometric shapes leading row on row, straight into the wall. I was dizzy again, but I stood up taller, looked forward. We were almost to the last door, to the sign that said, Welcome to the West. Through the thick walls, I could hear it—the storm growing stronger, the wind picking up speed.

I was hurrying, trying not to picture Sandra flying end on end out of the parking lot when I heard it—a sound cutting through the wind, overriding Nancy, who was starting to cry, who sniffled methodically with each step. I didn't say anything, though; I just squeezed her hand tighter and broke into a run.

We pushed through the last door, and I heard it again, and she was there—Rochelle cannonballing into the center of the pool, throwing up a giant splash—and my heart slowed, some.

The pool was framed by a wall of glass, window on top of window. I saw Sandra's reflection in the glass before I saw her—my niece hanging on the edge of the pool, kicking her legs, squealing. It took me a second to realize it was her, not some optical illusion, a second more to feel the water on my face, another still to realize I had not let go of Nancy's hand.

Rochelle, Nancy yelled, letting go, jumping into the pool, clothes and all, crying and laughing and hiccupping all at the same time.

Sandra grinned up at me. Hey, she said. Her grin wavered. Are we in trouble?

I tried to answer but everything felt frozen, and her smile unraveled further. She looked so much like her mother in that moment, with fear creeping into her face, that mine began to thaw.

No, I said, of course you're not in trouble.

I crouched next to her, was reaching down to touch the top of her head when I felt her hand on my back, and I started to fall, end on end into the pool. My face hit first and then my fists, which loosened on impact. The water was warmer than I would have guessed, and I stayed under, squinting against the chlorine sting, but I kept my eyes cracked, anyway. I spread out my limbs. My legs kicked and arms circled, and I headed for the center of the pool, down and down, till I reached the rough, concrete bottom.

I turned over to face the top. Above me, legs kicked fast and water churned. Nancy and the girls were laughing, but it all sounded slowed down like I was hearing it long after or just before it happened. I started to rise into the sound, but my arms fanned out further, and I kept myself there, waving my arms back and forth, which was a little like flying, a little like its opposite.

By the time I surfaced, Sandra and Nancy were laughing and high-fiving each other, and Nancy came swimming over to me. Her hair was matted to her face and gave off a powerful hairspray stench, and she was smiling.

Welcome, she said.

To the West? I said.

To the sixth grade, she said.

Other than her words and the splashing, it was quiet, peaceful. Outside, the storm was letting up a little now, the wind dying down, the sun coming through the thick barrier of clouds.

Inside, the water was keeping us warm, and I was comfortable there, maybe for the first time, even in my wet clothes. I thought about swimming to the edge, about pulling myself up. I thought about looking for the others, for Grandma Claw and our ceremony, but it seemed enough to splash and squeal and watch the snow come down outside the glass. It fell a little more softly and thickly than before, weighing down the small pines, settling into the half-filled holes, already starting to melt.

Song or Something Like It

Christmas Eve, two in the afternoon, three hours to go till church, when my brother Paul pulls out a snack-sized Ziploc of cocaine and a pen cap, the end removed. He spills it out onto the table between a tower of Bud Light cans and a plastic Christmas village, complete with skating rink. Our mother plugged in the village before she left to pick up our grandmother, who no longer drives after dark. It will be dark in a few hours. It already is dark in the village. The lights in the houses have been turned on, and they glow behind the skaters who figure eight in fits and starts out front on the plastic pond.

Here we go, Paul says. He's leaning forward, looking at me like he wants to launch into something, the coke, maybe, or one of his stories. The ones he loves most involve holidays, and the top three involve me trying to kill him. I tell myself we're not making Story Number Four; I tell myself there will be no Christmas tragedy, but Paul does the line anyway, shakes his head, makes a sound not unlike yee haw.

What is this, I say, A Very Hillbilly Christmas?

We may have a few hillbilly relatives somewhere on our mother's side, but mostly, we're métis, Roubideaux—a mixture of French and Blackfoot, trappers and traders. Mostly, yee haw is inappropriate.

Paul's been out checking the traps he set yesterday and is wearing long underwear and overalls, one strap unhooked. He smells like raccoon bait—the warm piss and week-old armpit combo sweetened slightly by the pot cloud that hangs over his head like dense fog. I can smell the chocolate-chip brownies Mom has made, too—Paul's favorites—and I'm focusing on that smell, its normalcy, trying to block out the others.

You have a problem with yee haw? Paul says.

His green eyes widen then narrow. He shakes his head, mock-frowns, and bursts into high-pitched giggles.

Our mother has frosted the insides of the windows, and it's hard to see in or out through the stippled snowmen and reindeer. They cast shadows on the table, or, in the tragedy, they do. In this false light, anything's possible. Paul could be twelve or thirteen, still making all his money from the trap line. We're returning from the river, the car trunk heavy with raccoons and coyotes. I'm letting him drive, though I know Dad won't like it, and Paul is hunched over the steering wheel, hands tight, face serious.

But that's not how it is, of course. Paul shakes his head so that his cheeks flap. The giggles rise again through the rotating fan to the top of the twelve-foot, vaulted ceiling. Paul's repeating it now like a chant—yee haw, yee haw, yee haw—trying to get me to smack him so he can smack me back.

Paul, I say, do you want the guests to hear?

This sends him giggling again, but at least the yee hawing stops. Our mother manages the only hotel in Talbot and lives behind it in a back house. The hotel is really an overgrown house—eight bedrooms with small bathrooms, a common room downstairs and a kitchen—ordinary. We know that now, but we grew up behind it, in the shadow of it and that phrase—Do you want the guests to hear? We were not allowed to be seen or heard by the guests, especially Dad and me, with our dark eyes, hair, and skin.

When Paul is four, once when Mom and Dad are fighting—Dad threatening quietly, Mom shouting—Paul sneaks up behind them, small fist on his hip, and in a perfect imitation of Mom, squeaks out, Do you want the guests to hear? Everyone laughs, a little louder than usual, even Mom, who shakes her head at Paul and tousles his light-brown hair like the moms do on television.

During our real, grown-up lives, Paul and I reside four hours north in the greater Minneapolis/St. Paul metropolitan area. I write technical manuals for a mid-size construction company, tracking the equipment. Paul works in business, moving from one store to the next, assistant managing, and he deals a little, too, on the side. When she is feeling proud of us, our mother likes to say we've come a long way from the trap line. When she is not, she says she can see the water on our shoes; she says she can smell the hides.

Paul drinks down the last of his Bud Light and adds it to the tower, which I am dismantling quietly, can by can, so as not to be noticed. He opens the nearest window, blows smoke out it.

A present, he says, for the guests.

Our mother's Christmas clock chimes, starts playing God Bless Ye Merry Gentlemen. Paul chair-dances to the music, his elbows jutting back and forth.

I sip from a glass of Diet Coke poured over ice, the can long since crushed and deposited in the pantry, in the blue bin marked CANS, ALUMINUM. There's also one for CANS, TIN, and it is yellow, of course, so there can be no confusion.

Alrighty, then, says Paul. Time to go to K-mart.

The first time I try to kill Paul, he is five, and I'm fifteen; it is the Fourth of July. We have taken our mother's car, have gone out to Big Lake to go swimming. We have just watched our father and grandfather get into the truck, back it out of the driveway, head it out onto the highway, going north on what they are calling a scouting mission. We are used to them being gone in the winter, but they are not supposed to leave us in the summer, on a summer holiday, no less. This is what I'm thinking as I wave after them, my hand going the wrong way, my hand saying, Come back. Paul chases the truck like a dog until he can no longer keep up, and I am ashamed for us all. Our mother goes into the hotel, back to the holiday guests, back to where we can't follow.

Most summers, after our father and I finish mowing lawns around town, we pick up Paul and go for long walks in the hills outside town. Our father tells us stories about up north, where Paul and I have never been, where our mother won't let us go. In the summer, we eat popsicles, holding them to our teeth to see who can stand the cold the longest. The winner gets the fourth popsicle, and I am always the winner. We eat the popsicles on the way to the lake, so that's what I do

today—I take our mother's car down the driveway, grab up
Paul, who is kicking and punching, and I buckle him into the
passenger seat despite both his fists grabbing and tangling my
hair. We head down Main Street to the only gas station, the
Get and Grab, and with the last of my lawn mowing money,
I buy us three popsicles. Paul refuses his, turns his head to
the window, so I open the popsicle for him, close his fist
around the stick.

They're not coming back, he says, are they.

It could be a question, but it is not, and, in any case, I don't
answer. I turn the radio up as loud as it goes, blaring a hair
metal song I will later be ashamed to have loved. I suck the
popsicle to my teeth, and soon Paul does the same. We drive
the three miles to the lake like that—the cold numbing our
teeth and mouths, the sticky runoff flooding our chins. I let
Paul win. We are at the lake when I hand him the last popsicle,
when he works his face into something that's supposed to be
a smile but is really more like a grimace.

I sit in our mother's car a while longer, shaking my head to
the music, and let Paul run ahead to pick our spot. But that's
not what Paul does. Instead, he throws his towel down on the
sand and heads straight for the water.

By the time I get there, it is all over. Later, this will be the
worst part—that I've missed it, that I only have the recon-
structed story, the horror of my own shame-induced imag-
inings—Paul swimming as furiously as he'd been running
earlier. Before long, Paul in the middle of the lake, his head
bobbing under.

A big girl from school swims out, pulls Paul to the shore.
She tilts his head and pushes on his chest until Paul retches

and gags up the popsicle warmed by lake water, a sticky red mess that worries the onlookers, that looks so much like blood they are sure he will die. But he doesn't, of course, and later, when he tells our mother the story, there is little emphasis on how far out he swam, much emphasis on the high drama, the near tragedy. How he was all by himself out there in the big lake. How he was left all alone to drown.

K-mart is its own version of tragedy. The parking lot is filled with cars parked haphazardly as if abandoned, front bumpers crossing lines, back ends sticking out. I can see their former occupants—haggard, stoop-shouldered parents shoving carts down aisle after aisle, some taking the corners on two wheels. We've driven twenty miles to get here, Paul behind the wheel, alternately zipping, then crawling past fallow cornfields, abandoned buildings, and clapboard farmhouses decked out in wreaths and lights.

The store closes in forty minutes, and we sit in Paul's car, his hands slack around the bong but tight on the lighter. He's forgotten his pipe, a small, ornate one-hitter, so he's using the Honey Bear, a bong made from a plastic, bear-shaped honey jar. He's been complaining of a cold, has filled the Honey Bear with apple juice.

You know, I say, your nose would run less if you'd stop putting shit up it.

He takes a hit.

Tangy, he says, yet sweet.

We enter K-mart with twenty-five minutes till closing. Paul insists on driving the cart, and he steers like he can't feel the cool metal bar under his hands. He is sweating a little around the hairline and on his upper lip, and when he reaches to wipe his face, he steers the cart out of Aisle One into a sale bin. The stuffed Santas in the cage cartwheel before falling.

So do we have a list? I say.

Teresa, Teresa, he says, tapping his forehead. It's all up here.

We turn the corner into Aisle Two, Cooking Utensils. I'm squinting into the fluorescent lights, studying the sign, wondering if there are *non-cooking* utensils, and when I look back, Paul and the cart are gone. I repeat to myself that we are fine. I repeat to myself that there will be no tragic end, but my mouth goes dry anyway, and my feet suddenly won't do anything but shuffle.

I stumble over to Aisle Three, Cookwares—no Paul—and notice a food dehydrator hanging on the edge of the second shelf. I grab it, continue to Aisle Four, Housewares. I scan Housewares, then Pets—still, no Paul. He's not in Sporting Goods, either, or Health and Beauty. I'm starting to sweat now, too, and with the crowd thinning out, the hum from the fluorescent lights makes my head hurt, all the blood rushing to my temples.

Welcome K-mart shoppers. The store will be closing in five minutes.

The nasal, adolescent voice drones on, lilting up at the ends of words like the boy is excited for Christmas or home or who knows what.

I lean against a display vacuum cleaner, cradle the food dehydrator under my chin, and then the nasal voice comes again—Security to Aisle Nine. Security to Aisle Nine.

My legs remember how to work, and I leave the vacuum

cleaner display, running past paper towels and watches, rounding Aisle Nine in step with a large man in tight, dark pants and a name badge.

Aisle Nine, Seasonals. Paul sits in a sale bin not unlike the one he bumped earlier, his feet dangling out over the cage's side, his overalled butt resting on dozens of small, fuzzy, reindeer. Paul looks like a lighter copy of our father—same square face, same upturned eyes. This is what I'm thinking, all I'm thinking, when Tight Pants advances on Paul.

A blue light blinks over Paul's head.

Again, Paul says, clapping. Again.

I step forward, put my arm on Tight Pants' sleeve, and he turns. Paul winks at me and I frown. I turn back to Tight pants, tap my finger to my temple, and shrug. A *what can you do* look passes from me to him, and he steps aside. It's Christmas, after all, and he lets me pull Paul out of the reindeer to the check-out. There is a part of me that has to stifle my own giggles, another part that is pure, raw fear. My head is tight, stretched, and I step quickly to keep up with Paul, who is all business now, moving fast to get in the shortest line.

Paul carries two reindeer up to the register, hanging on to their back legs, antlers bumping against the rough weave of his overalls. I hand him the food dehydrator, which he sits on the conveyor belt, tracking all three as if they might escape.

For Mom, he says. Very good.

I nod, resist the urge to ask what Grandma and I are supposed to do with stuffed reindeer.

It is 4:15. We're the last car on this side of the K-Mart parking lot, and the safety lights above us click off as we reach the car. Paul calls our mother, cell phone to cell phone, though she's home from picking up Grandma by now. They're sitting at the table—Grandma's sharp eyes narrowing at the spectacle of the decorations, Mom's hands moving in and out fast, chain smoking, jabbing the air when she tells Paul to tell me to hurry, when she curses me under her breath for not having delivered him home on time.

This time, I drive. The reindeer lie at Paul's feet, their heads poking out of the plastic bag, dark, dull eyes looking up at the Honey Bear, which rides shotgun with Paul. My hands on the steering wheel shake a little, but my feet are still enough to keep the car at a regular rhythm. The farmhouses and cornfields pass by at an even clip, many of them now lit up in flashing red and green, so the landscape seems to be blinking and nodding.

We pass the turnoff for the river, the trap line, and I slow the car for a moment, but there is not enough time to stop for the raccoon and otter who wait, their feet snared, their bodies stuck at the water's edge, in that in between place—bank and river, silence and cold.

The car's steady hum has lulled Paul into sleep. His head is tilted back against the window, his mouth hanging open a little. The sun is setting behind Paul, and from where I sit, it seems to be dropping into his mouth, down and down, splashing red.

The second time I try to kill Paul, he is six, and I'm sixteen. Our father has come back but is not back in any way that matters. It is almost fall, is Labor Day weekend, the mowing season nearly ended. Still, our father leaves for work in the morning before I'm awake, comes home after I'm sleeping, though I try to stay up, looking at ceiling shadows that could be fish, could be clouds. There have been no popsicles all summer, just silence, stale and long and in danger of becoming permanent. It has been a summer of me wanting my privacy, of Paul wanting to be around me.

I am on the phone with Gail, one of my best friends, when I hear a wailing coming from the back porch, not ten feet away. I sigh into the phone and hold it out for Gail. Can you believe him? I say. He'll try anything.

We laugh. The day before when we'd talked on the phone, Paul had bounced a basketball in the kitchen until I'd had to hang up.

Shut up, I yell out to the porch. Shut up, shut up, shut up.

We go on like that, Gail and I talking, Paul wailing, me shouting. I'm tied to the dining room by the plastic spirals of the cord, am laughing with Gail, sighing then shouting each time a wail sounds from the porch. Gail plays me a new Blondie song, and we're listening together, imitating the scratchy voice, laughing. The wailing is regular now, low under Blondie like dissonance. Another minute passes before I decide I'd better go make Paul stop. Blondie is nearing the end, is wailing one last time, and there, on the porch is Paul—Paul moaning out his dissonance, Paul in a circle of his own blood.

It has rained hard the night before, the weather turning cool and wet early, the temperature hovering around freezing. Paul has been over at a neighbor boy's house, has been climbing the oak tree next to the metal shed, has been climbing high enough to catch the thick branch over the shed's roof. Paul and his friend take turns climbing, shimmying out onto the branch, crouching, then standing, then swinging down at a hard angle onto the roof where the water has pooled and slicked.

Paul vaults himself higher and slides further with each try, until his friend says, Hey, man, and I'm getting cold, and Maybe we should go in.

But Paul doesn't hear him. Paul hears the sound of our father's truck, rumbling and stalling down the driveway each morning. Paul feels how his bedroom window grows cooler with each passing day, sees how his breath steams the glass, feels how this will be the end of summer before it really even began.

On the last climb, the last swing and vault, Paul is imagining himself up north with the rest of the men—he is imagining himself dark and grown and strong—he is yelling, mouth open wide. And then his feet are nearing the edge, then over, his hands reaching for the roof's edge but missing, the shed's door leaning half open, Paul reaching and falling, falling and reaching, until he finds the door, his mouth making first contact, the sharp, metal corner meeting his upper lip, tearing.

But I don't learn this until later. When I find him bleeding on the porch, he is leaning against the cool, metal railing. His hair sticks up in the front and dangles, lank, down his neck in the back, as is the fashion. His eyes are far away, still up north, maybe, or looking for a place where there is no pain. I can't tell where the blood is coming from but can see drops of it in the yard leading to the steps, can see it's coming from Paul. The noise is coming from him, too, and though it sounds like a faker's noise, I understand now it is the opposite—that its otherworldly quality is from pain, not an attempt to irritate or underscore Blondie.

I retreat into the house to call our mother, hearing her voice already, how I should have been watching. How Paul is my responsibility. How I left Paul all alone.

The hotel out front is quiet and dark, except for its halo of gold lights and the pastiche on the front lawn—rotating reindeer and a red-faced Santa who cradles a bright, shiny package.

We're home, I say.

Paul jerks awake, rubs his eyes with the back of his hand. Mom's house is dark, too, but she's left the tree lit in the living room. From our position in the car, the house looks like a half-hearted tragedy has begun, like part of it has caught fire—some sort of red-gold, slow-moving fire that never seems to make it past the living room.

Paul has his keys out, fumbling and dropping them twice before I try the door, which Mom has left unlocked. So I'm the first one in. I'm the one who flips on the kitchen lights and sees it. I'm the one who takes a step back.

I freeze in the doorway, and Paul gives me a shove. I step aside, let him move in front of me, and then he sees it.

Jesus, Paul says. His voice is hushed, respectful.

We're both in the kitchen doorway, my hand still on the knob, and Paul is rubbing his eyes again with the back of his other hand.

Yeah, I say, Jesus.

On the top of Mom's brand new, Whirlpool Gold stove lies the pan of chocolate-chip brownies, Paul's favorites. Mom saved for two years for this stove, raved to Paul and me about its grill-like surface capabilities, its precision baking accuracy. There is heat still radiating from the precision oven, so the brownies must have been left to cool, must still be warm.

But this has not deterred the squirrel, whose considerable tail switches back and forth on top of the grill-like surface, whose feet and haunches rest on top of Paul's brownies. To call this thing a squirrel is not really accurate, is not precise. Squirrels are small and fuzzy—cute in a rat-cousin sort of way. This thing easily weighs three pounds. Its fur sticks up on top of its head like it's been electrified, like it has only recently come back to life.

Its back legs and haunches are sinking into the brownies. Paul and I both gasp and step back a little as it scoots its butt around, getting comfortable, surveying us with its beady eyes like we're the ones out of place.

The window, Paul says. He lights a cigarette and shakes his head, grinning weakly.

The window in the dining room is wide open, like we left it, and the ashtray on the dining room table is overturned. Some of the ash has migrated to the plastic Christmas village, toward the forest, the pond, and the skaters, who have been left turned on. They circle and spin, the one at the edge jerking back and forth in one spot, graceless, obstructed by a cigarette butt that, in different light, could be a log. I look above the skaters to the village, to where the houses loom, where there could be a volcano.

The ash and cigarette butts spill out from the village onto the chairs and hardwood floor, mixing with the thin layer of dust to make a haphazard trail into the kitchen, to the stove, to the brownies.

My gun's in the car, Paul says. But he's moving forward even as he says it. He's taken off his coat and has picked up a candy cane, is holding it out in front of himself like a staff.

The squirrel reclines further into the brownies. A half-melted chocolate chip lingers in its whiskers, and its tongue flicks sideways, the chip just out of reach.

The next part is a flurry of motion and countermotion—Paul feigning left with the candy cane, the squirrel skidding right, plowing a crooked furrow through a brownie row. Paul's swing somehow anticipates what happens next—the giant squirrel coming to the edge of the pan, the pan tipping, the squirrel off balance. And the coat is there, unlikely but there just the same, swooping down over that awful, electrified head. And then Paul, the coat, the squirrel underneath spinning and stumbling out the door—the coat twitching and jumping under Paul's arm, the squirrel skittering down Paul's leg to the floor, the squirrel running out the door. And then the door jumps shut behind them, and I'm alone with the skaters, the massacred brownies.

I scoop up the disaster, pan and all, and dump it into the trash, which I tie shut. I wet a paper towel and move to the dining room, where I wipe the skaters clean. I'm holding the ashy paper towel in one hand, the cigarette butt in the other, and I move to the window. I'm focusing on the small details like keeping all the ash in the paper towel.

The air from the window pushes against me, and I'm cold, colder than I ever remember being. The window is cold, too, is frozen open, maybe, and in any case, it won't move.

Outside, Paul looks colder than I feel. He is standing at the bottom of the oak tree closest to the hotel. He is standing there with his coat on the ground beside him, his pipe in one hand, the candy cane in the other. Mom's clock begins Angels We Have Heard on High, and I call out to Paul. I say,

We're going to tell Mom you ate the brownies. I say, They were good—you enjoyed them. The clock voices break into the first of the glorias, and I say, We're going to be late for church, and I want you to stop. I say the last part over and over, my voice small and high, not unlike the sound an animal makes in a snare that's pulled too tight. But the window has come loose, is sliding down, and Paul's face is turning, not toward me, but to the tree, up to where I imagine the squirrel has gone. The hotel's Santa display lights Paul's face in gold, then red, then leaves it in shadow. I lean my forehead against the cool of the glass, the second round of clock-voice glorias coming on bright and false and strong.

The third time I try to kill Paul it is Thanksgiving. He is eight, and I'm eighteen, am waiting tables six miles from home at a Happy Chef diner off the Interstate. I'm saving my tips for college, for escape. Our father is gone for what will be the last time, and though we don't know this yet for certain, we feel it.

The diner is packed with middle-aged women in holiday sweatshirts, turkeys in tall hats and sequins dancing across sagging breasts and thickening middles. One of the waitresses has called in sick, and we are short-staffed, the other waitress and I running from table to booth to table, tired smiles stretching our faces. Paul has come along to clear tables, or this is what we've told our mother, anyway.

Mostly, Mom is busy with the holiday guests, too busy to see what I see—the look on Paul's face when she checks on our turkey, the smallest any of us has ever seen, when he counts the plates at the table, once, twice, three times, coming up short, wrong, each time.

When my shift starts at nine, we really do need Paul's help, the place packed with holiday travelers. Paul swoops around, removing plates and filling water glasses, everyone smiling at him because he is eight years old, his face all scrunched and serious. By two o'clock, though, the flood of customers has slowed to an odd couple or two, desperate to use the restrooms, ordering pie or coffee before hurrying back out onto the Interstate, trying to get to where they're going on time. Later, I will blame those people, the tired look of holiday purpose on their faces—that almost-home look—and what it does to Paul, who is watching from a corner booth, having finished some turkey and instant mashed potatoes, having drunk his second cup of milky, overly sugared coffee.

I go out back for a cigarette with Marlene, the other waitress. We stay out there too long, laughing over the woman who forgot her purse in the restroom, her coat on the back of her chair, her to-go-box on the counter by the register. When we come back in, Paul's booth is empty, as is the restaurant. The only sounds are the methodical scrape, scrape of the cooks cleaning the grills, the wind rattling the windows on the north side of the building.

I joke around with Marlene some more, steal a Junior Mint for my breath, and start on my side work—filling catsup bottles and wiping down salt and pepper shakers. Every minute or so I glance over to the booth where Paul had been sitting. I'm thinking he's in the bathroom, that he's been in there a long time. I have not forgotten him, which is what he will say later, but still, it takes me too long to pay attention to the tightness that starts in my belly, longer still before I knock on the bathroom door, then enter, then rush out again, through the dinging door into the cold outside, without a word to Marlene, unable to speak even if I'd thought to.

The day had started out cloudy, a storm threatening, but now is bitter cold and bright, the sun sharp and false overhead. Paul is not in the parking lot or leaning against the car, waiting. I scan the horizon—the Interstate stretched out, north/south, into the flat, brown landscape, the cars and trucks and semis winding and climbing the only hill in sight. And it is there that I see Paul, moving up the only hill, the cold wind blowing back his hair, his fists at his sides pumping, propelling him north.

Even today, in our grown-up lives, when I think of Paul, this is how I see him first—so slight against the wind, so cold under that bright, useless sky.

I have to cross the southbound traffic to reach him. It is not as difficult as it could be, and it all happens in the focused but distilled time of important moments—my legs carrying me to the ditch, waiting one, two, three seconds for the last semi, entering that lane, one, two seconds more to wait before running through the space between a pickup and a station wagon. No one honks, or if they do, I don't notice. I hadn't thought to get my coat, and my uniform is a short-sleeved dress, but I don't feel the cold either—that will come later. For now, there is the crunch of hoar frost grass under my feet, the sun in my eyes, and my hand coming up to make a shield, to keep Paul in sight.

When I reach him, he is at the top of the hill. He is leaning on his knees to catch his breath. He is wearing his coat but no gloves, and this is what comes out of me—Where are your gloves?—as I pull him to me, as we fall to our knees on the cold, damp ground.

I don't know, Paul says. I don't.

His eyes are tired, used up. He stares past me at the north-
bound lane, and we sit like that a while, the symphony of the
traffic around us, the both of us trying our very best to stay
quiet and small and still.

The Christmas Eve service at the church will differ little from
the K-mart—same parents, same children, just in pews instead
of aisles—but now the parents' faces will have gone past frantic
to tired. Some, even, will be trying on *happy* or *jolly* or the
closest they can manage. I know all this—it's the same every
year—but still I pull Paul from underneath the tree. Still we
begin the short walk to the church.

Paul's face is tired, too, serious and purposeful. I have to
take two strides for each of his, and he swings his arms faster
and faster like we're racing. He's clutching the candy cane, his
eyes elsewhere, focused on something other than this place,
and I know it's not me he's hurrying to or from.

The churchyard holds a display similar to the hotel's, only
with a Mary, three wise men, and the baby Jesus instead of
a Santa. Mary looks down at Jesus with an expression that's
supposed to be beneficent, I would guess, only she's in Technicolor, flashing blues and reds and golds that stop at her
neckline, that leave her eyes and face lifeless.

Behind Mary is the stained glass, and beyond the stained
glass, the church's guts—the worn pews, the hymnals, the
hushed lighting. I stand between Mary and a small snow drift,
the product of someone thoughtfully shoveling off Mary and
her friends but being too tired, maybe, to carry the weight
of the snow much further. The drift rises up between Mary

and the window, making a lopsided obstacle that threatens to avalanche down, to cover everything.

Paul skims the top of the drift, packs the snow into a hard ball he pretends to aim at me. I pretend to be scared, ducking down. He lets the snow fly, out into the silent street, where it skids and comes to rest on the center line.

There will be no mention of the squirrel, I say. I'm laughing a little as I say it, and Paul is almost smiling.

We forgot to check the traps, he says. My fault.

We can do it later, I say. Later is soon enough.

I make my voice light, trying to will a good mood. My hand is on the church door, and Paul is right behind me, is nodding and almost smiling, but when I turn, he is back at the manger. I shade my eyes against Mary's Technicolor glow, and Paul is bending down, is on one knee in front of Mary and the baby Jesus, has his head next to Mary's. Paul is looking at Jesus like he has a question he can't quite remember.

I move back to Paul, stand between him and the baby Jesus. It's time, I say. I put my hand on Paul's shoulder, and we turn toward the church. Paul comes back to himself, his purpose, and he's opening the door, is through it before he realizes I'm not behind him.

It's so quiet outside that I can hear him inside, stomping the snow from his shoes. I can hear the squeak he makes on the inside stairs. I move to the stained glass window behind Mary, stand next to the drift. The church is as I remembered—full of tired parents and excited children, and I'm sure it still smells like an old person's attic. Paul is going to have to sit in the only spot left, in the back pew by the door, next to the old married couple who hand out the programs. They whisper greetings and hug him as he enters.

The fourth time I try to kill Paul, he is twenty-three and I'm thirty-three. It is Christmas Eve, and he is entering the church. The old couple gives him a program and a candle, holding his hands longer than necessary, pretending not to notice his sweating. Paul looks behind him, to make a face at me, but I'm not there, and for a brief moment, he sees what this means. It is there in his face, the straightening of his lips, the new sweat along the hairline—how he will be in sharp focus during the prayer, Christmas dinner, the opening of presents. How he will have to answer the questions: Where's your sister? What did you do?

I'm willing my feet backward, am trying to pull my face away from the glass, but I see how frozen he is, how still, even through this window—everything tinted, red, green, gold. I try to stop myself, but I can't. I'm moving forward, the old oak doors swinging open and creaking shut behind me, my feet squeaking up the inside stairs, and then Paul turns, letting a breath go. I take a candle in one hand and steady Paul's arm, his shaking candle, with my other hand. I see he still has the candy cane, too, is gripping it tight.

For a moment, we are the only ones standing, awkward, out of place, but neither of us moves. Up front, more candles are being lit, and then the lights are dimmed. We should take our seats now, do something, but we hang there a moment longer, candle-lit, near the exit, suspended.

Paul opens his mouth, but no words come. I want him to say he's sorry, and I want to say it, too. I want to say I should have done more. I want to say I'll never leave.

We are saved by the music starting up, by everyone rising, collective. Paul grabs a hymnal from the closest pew, and I find the right page. The organ belts out Silent Night so loud it makes me wince, but Paul doesn't seem to notice. He is focusing on the hymnal, the words, and so I do the same.

Tomorrow, we'll check the trap lines. Tomorrow, it will be Christmas. Tomorrow, we will think of our father, the good times, the opposite of tragedy. But for now, we are here, together, moving our mouths along in song or something like it, and our candles raise shadows like fingers that stretch across the walls, across the stained-glass windows. We are together, we are together, and those shadows are reaching out and burning and reaching out again.

In the Native Storiers series:

Mending Skins
by Eric Gansworth

Designs of the Night Sky
by Diane Glancy

From the Hilltop
by Toni Jensen

Bleed into Me: A Book of Stories
by Stephen Graham Jones

Hiroshima Bugi: Atomu 57
by Gerald Vizenor

Native Storiers: Five Selections
edited and with an introduction
by Gerald Vizenor

Elsie's Business
by Frances Washburn

To order or obtain more information
on these or other University of
Nebraska Press titles, visit
www.nebraskapress.unl.edu